CRASH KITTY

CRASH KITTY

an OFF MY FEET

origins story

rachel tremblay

This is a work of fiction. Names, characters, businesses, places, events, locales, and incidents are either the products of the author's imagination or used in a fictitious manner. Any resemblance to actual persons, living or dead, or actual events is purely coincidental.

ISBN: 978-0-9690172-8-8

E-BOOK: 978-1-7771061-0-2

GrindSpark Press

www.rachel-tremblay.com

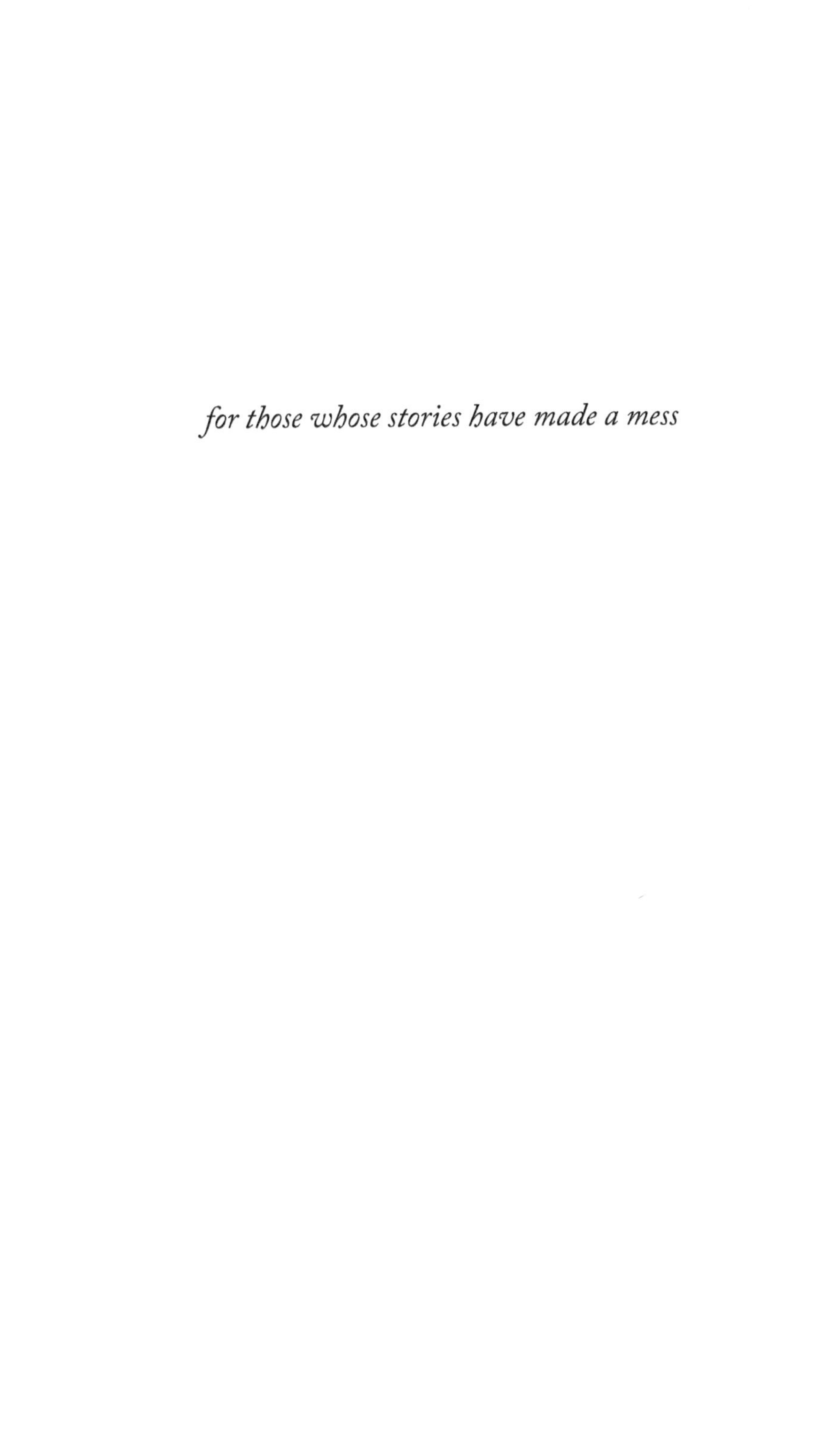

for those whose stories have made a mess

Bloody Beach Sugar Sex Magic

"This is a dumb idea," Maddy said, her hand stretched out over the crystal bowl that sat in the centre of the coffee table.

"What if one of us has a disease, yet to be discovered?"

That was Lo, the hypochondriac. It was surprising she was going through with it at all. Even now, her hand quivered above the bowl.

Sitting on the edge of one of the two couches was Bee, whose job was to puncture the fingertips with a triple-disinfected needle.

But the idea was Kat's, and she told everyone to suck it up.

"Besides, I love you all so much, I'm ready to share any of your weirdo germs." Kat took a swig from her beer and slid up closer to Bee, kissing her on the cheek. She offered her hand, palm upwards, and grinned.

"*Ow!*"

"You want to bleed? Well, it's not going to tickle," said Bee, proceeding to make a dimple in her own fingertip. The skin pierced with a soft *pop*, a bubble of blood blossoming on the surface. "Okay girls, this is it."

Arms extended, the four young women looked at each other, a nervous energy passing from one gaze to the next. They were just messing around, they all knew that, but there was an eerie vibe to their little ceremony, a seriousness that transcended the bonds of school, work, and childhood. This ritual would make them family.

Lights dimmed, candles glowing orange among the bottles and glasses of leftover wine placed like chess pieces around the crimson-streaked bowl—it was perfect.

John Mayer crooned from the sound system, the volume low enough that he might actually have been locked in the broom closet, serenading them full-heartedly, desperately trying to push his charm through the door.

"What do we do now?" asked Lo in a whisper, her eyes saucer-round.

"We stick our fingers together where they were pricked so that we come into contact with each other's blood. It's dumb," repeated Maddy.

"It's *poetic*," corrected Kat, shooting a sideways glance at Maddy. "This way, whatever happens, we'll always have part of each other within us."

The others nodded, their smiles fading as they remembered Claire, who had died the year before after being struck by a mango truck.

"Fuck mangoes," said Bee quietly.

"Fuck mangoes!" they responded in unison, and pushed their fingertips together in a bloody kiss. Lo started crying, and that was that.

"Oh, baby," said Kat, crawling over to the couch opposite and wrapping her arms around Lo's shoulders. The other two blew out the candles and flicked on the lights, then sank back with their drinks, the thrill over and done with.

"Let John out of the closet, will ya?" Maddy said to Bee, who had the remote beside her. She cranked it until his luscious whining overpowered Lo's weeping. The girls sang along, Lo finally joining in for the chorus, her beer bottle now a microphone.

The song ended and Bee turned the volume back down. "Back in the closet you go."

"You know, I don't know why he has to make that face when he plays his guitar," said Maddy.

Bee laughed. "Come on, Maddy, he plays like a god. He's blowing his *own* mind."

"Or holding his guitar a little too snug," said Kat, pointing to her crotch, her eyebrows popping up and down. "He's really *feeling* it."

Giggles chimed likes bells in the small living room, bouncing against the bottles, the framed Led Zeppelin and Cream posters, the glass patio doors.

"I find it makes him less credible," continued Maddy. "Like he needs to convince us that he's really that good."

Kat came back to her spot on the couch beside Bee. "But he *is* good. So it doesn't matter—we're convinced either way."

"Are we, though?"

"I think Kat's right," said Bee. "He's *turned on* as hell. That is clearly his sex face."

They all howled.

"Fuck it, let him back out, poor bastard," said Kat. They turned the music back up and danced in the dining area (which had no table and was reserved for such shenanigans), playing air guitar and making sex faces as they sang along.

Bee bobbed over to the kitchen to make herself a drink.

"Make me one?" came Kat's slurred voice from behind. "Your bloody sunshine on the beach."

Bee turned and, seeing Kat's crooked smile, rolled her eyes. "That's not what it's called. And no."

"Why not?"

"You'll throw up."

"No, I won't."

"I'll make it virgin."

"It'll take a lot more than your crazy made-up drink to make me a virgin." Kat hopped her butt onto the counter, only to slip immediately back off and flop to the ground. The loud thud drew Maddy and Lo to the scene, who, upon seeing Kat sprawled out on the kitchen floor, burst into laughter so violent they shook like bags of hot, popping corn.

Kat was pulled to her feet and all four stumbled back to the living room, murmuring giggles and exulted sighs.

"I dare you to drink that down in one shot!" said Kat, nodding at Bee's drink.

"What are we, in high school?" Maddy shook her head.

Bee held up her glass to Kat and, after surveying her crowd with a dignified frown, downed it—but slowly, because the thing tasted good.

"Bloody beach sugar sex magic!" she gasped, wiping her mouth with the back of her hand. "I'm going to be rich. All right, then. My turn."

"Your turn for what?" said Kat.

Bee held a finger to her lips, then pointed it to Lo. "I dare you, Lo, to throw your bra out the window."

Lo tsk-ed. "We live so dangerously."

"We take candy from strangers!" Kat threw her arms up.

Lo reached behind her back, fiddled with the clasp, tugged here and there, and pulled a pink lace bra out through her shirt sleeve. The others followed her to the balcony, giggling.

The apartment was six stories high, the building's last, and the people below were far enough that they looked small, but not so small that you couldn't throw a rock at them if you wanted to. It was eleven, and Friday nightlife was bustling.

"You need to toss it out far if you want it to land on someone," instructed Maddy.

Lo bent over the railing, Kat and Bee holding her by the waist in case she toppled. Dangling from her fingertips, the flimsy piece of cloth swung back and forth as she tried to give it momentum. Finally, she swung and, with a grunt, hurled it into the night, her upper body tipping forward with it. Fingernails dug into her skin as the girls held onto her, though they couldn't help following the bra down with their eyes. Being lace, it had no weight to it, and caught in the wind before whipping back towards the building, landing on a balcony a few stories below. A head popped out, and then a hand clutching the pink bra victoriously. The girls hooted and hollered, to which the guy holding the bra looked up and smiled.

"Hi!" he called.

The girls laughed, waved, and retreated.

"Oh, you guys, you clawed me good," said Lo, rubbing her flanks. "I'll need some alcohol for that."

Maddy passed her a bottle of Jack Daniel's.

"Not that kind, you jerk." Lo laughed her way to the bathroom and came back with some rubbing alcohol and cotton swabs. "Okay, my turn. Maddy."

"Yes?"

"You're going to call Jack."

Maddy pointed to her bottle of liquor quizzically, raising an eyebrow.

"No," said Lo slowly. "Work Jack. You're going to confess your love for him."

"Shit, we *are* back in high school. Look, this is the only Jack I need in my life."

"Ya, right," said Kat. "You won't shut up about him. *Jack's got great hands, Jack's so funny, I want to climb up a tree with Jack and bone.* Anyway, you have to take the dare, Maddy. It's the rules."

Maddy threw up her arms, the whiskey bottle flailing. "What rules? I didn't agree to this."

"The blood thing," said Bee. "We did the blood thing. Now, you take the dare."

"You guys suck." Maddy took a swig of her preferred Jack and then reached for the cordless phone on the end table. She dialled and waited. It rang once, twice, three times. Her smile grew as the rings continued.

"He's not there," she told the girls, her smile by now a wide, smug grin.

"Maddy?"

"Oh, crap." Maddy almost dropped the phone. "Err, yes, hi Jack. It's Madeleine. I have to warn you, I'm drunk, and I'll fully regret this on Monday morning, if I remember any of it. If I don't remember, please play along and forget I ever said anything."

"Okay?"

"I … you …."

The girls snickered.

"Shut up! Damn it." She turned back to the phone. "Anyway, Jack, you're, well—you're one heck of a guy."

The girls laughed even louder. *"One heck of a guy!"* Kat howled.

"Come on, guys! Pipe down!"

"What's going on over there? Are you having a party?" asked Jack.

"Not really. It's just the girls and me."

"The girls?"

"Ya. Look, I have a stupid crush on you, that's all I'm going to say. This is dumb. Bye." She hung up, cheeks throbbing pink.

"Damn, that's going to hurt in the morning!" said Kat, wheezing with delight.

Maddy, still blushing, muttered something into her whiskey bottle. Kat poured another glass of wine.

Bee, still choking back giggles, stood and headed for the kitchen. She re-emerged with another homemade drink for herself and a beer for Lo. "It's your turn, Maddy," she said.

Maddy looked up. "Who's left?"

"Me," said Kat.

"Ha! Kat, you little fox. You wanna play schoolyard games, I'm throwing it to you old school. I dare you to kiss"—Maddy looked at the girls—"Bee. *With* the tongue."

Lo squealed. Bee and Kat, side by side on the couch, looked at one another.

"I give you my permission," said Bee, turning to face Kat and closing her eyes. Kat licked her lips, swallowed hard, and inched closer.

"Do you all have to watch?" she asked.

"Of course!" said Maddy. "That's the whole point, isn't it? It's just a kiss. Don't be a baby."

"I guess, but this is Bee."

Bee waited, eyes still closed. "Come on, Kat." She puckered up. Kat slipped her hands behind Bee's neck and pushed her lips against Bee's. They both opened their mouths in obedience to the dare, their tongues dancing—uncomfortably at first, but the heat rose quickly and they held each other tighter, the kiss deep and long.

"Whoaaaa," said Lo and Maddy, both mesmerized. Bee finally pulled away, panting.

"Damn alcohol," said Kat, shaking her head. She straightened her clothes, seeking composure by means of a deep breath. Bee said nothing, her cheeks flushed and her gaze dropping to the bottles on the table.

"John, where are you?" Kat called suddenly, an edge of irritation to her voice. She reached for the remote, stretching over Bee's lap, who watched her closely. The volume pumped up and the girls relaxed into the song.

"Gosh, he's so yummy," said Maddy.

"Hey, you can't have them all, Maddy. You have Jack, leave us John," said Kat.

"The sex faces, though," said Lo.

"All right, all right," said Maddy, who was trying very hard to look sober, straightening herself up and putting on sophisticated airs. "We played dare. But that's a child's game. How about something a little more risky?"

Lo frowned. "What's riskier than dare?"

"Truth." She smiled.

Just Like in the Movies

Maddy stretched out, purring, and thrust her feet onto the table, knocking over a half-full bottle of beer. "Fuck," she said, stumbling to her feet and tottering out of the room. She reappeared with two rolls of paper towel and fell to her knees beside the spill. Pushing scrunched-up towel into the sodden carpet, she smiled at Bee and nodded for her to begin.

"Me? Oh, okay. Let's see." Bee looked at the girls one by one. "Lo, who's your favourite?"

"My favourite what?"

"Your favourite out of us three."

Kat hissed, disapproving.

"You can't ask that!" said Lo. "That's just cruel."

"*We* are playing truth. And *you* need to answer because that. Is. The. Rule," urged Maddy, happy to be calling the shots at last. She took the drenched balls of towel from under her knees, threw them across the room into the kitchen, and climbed back onto the couch.

"Okay, fine, but if all hell breaks loose with you bitches, you asked for it. I love you all, with all my heart, but my favourite is …" Lo waited, watching them squirm in their seats. It was a silly game, that was all. It didn't mean anything. They'd all forget come morning time. "Kat."

"I knew it!" shouted Kat, who jumped to the opposite couch and put her arms, and one leg, around Lo, shoving her face into her neck and kissing her repeatedly. She pulled her face out of Lo's hair. "Maddy, trade."

Maddy got up and changed couches to sit beside Bee. They looked at each other, pouting.

"So, are you going to tell us why?" asked Maddy.

"Why she's my favourite, or why you're not?" said Lo.

"Why she's your favourite! I'm not in the mood for self-pity."

"Because she truly cares about people. And she's courageous. I like that. Plus, she always smells awesome."

"Aw, baby Lo," said Kat, squeezing her tighter.

"Well, I guess it's my turn, then," said Lo, ignoring Kat's groping. "The one who will answer my question is Bee. Bee, what is your deepest, darkest, secret fear? Something big—something you've never told anyone."

"Man does this game ever suck," said Bee. She thought for a while, poking at the ice in her drink with her straw. The silence didn't seem to bother anyone. Maddy was scribbling something on a piece of paper on the edge of the coffee table, and Lo was picking at the corners of her beer's label. Kat was lying back, staring at the ceiling, a faraway look in her eyes.

"Okay," Bee said at last. "I've got something. It's dark, but that's what you want, right? Here goes." She took a deep breath. "I am afraid that I will live my whole life without ever getting my parents' approval and that they will die without ever being proud of me. I'm afraid they will never see me as more than a dropout, a quitter, a loser, a failed daughter, and that I will live my life trying to do things to impress them without ever seeing those things through because I'm too fucking scared that I'll fail at those too, which would just make them hate me even more. So I'll stay at my dead-end job, date my dead-beat boyfriends, drink myself stupid every weekend with my enabling girlfriends, and risk never amounting to anything. That's my fear. But I love you so much, guys, please don't ever leave me—I swear I'll die."

She slurped through the straw, her glass empty, pushing the ice around to get the last drops. When she looked up, Lo's eyes were filled with tears, and Maddy and Kat were staring, mouths slightly agape.

"Okay, my turn," said Bee.

Maddy blanched. "Wait, what? We're not just going to move on after that! We need to talk about this!"

"Like hell we do! I answered the question. I'm fine with it. Not my problem if you aren't. Sorry, Lo."

Lo wiped the tears from her cheeks.

"My question is for Kat," said Bee.

"Ready, I think," answered Kat, frowning.

"Do you like women?"

"Like, in the way I think you're asking?"

"Exactly that way."

Kat grinned. "It was a good kiss, wasn't it, Bee babe?"

"Just answer the question."

"Why, you want to *do it* with me?"

"You're so full of yourself," said Bee. She rolled her eyes, toying with the straw between her teeth.

"Well, if you must know, no. I like bananas, not peaches. Though I could definitely make exceptions. I mean, a soul is a soul, a mouth is a mouth. A pretty face, a funny laugh—what's not to love about that?"

"So, you like both?"

"That's two questions, *madame*! I'm afraid it's *my* turn." Kat poured herself more wine, her eyes narrowing as she tried very hard to avoid spilling any over the rim. Satisfied, she plucked up the glass, swirled it, sniffed it, and laughed. "I can't smell anything. Okay. Who's left. Madeleine." She looked at Maddy, who was across from her, still scribbling on her paper.

"What are you writing there?" she asked.

"An idea for a short story. Hey, that was a question! You wasted your question!" Maddy stood up and did a little dance, bumping her hips side to side as she chanted, *"You wasted your question, you wasted your question!"*

Kat snorted. "Fine, whatever. Can we hear it?"

Maddy stopped dancing with a start and sat. "Well, it's not done."

"Doesn't matter. Read what you have so far."

"Um, okay." Maddy rubbed her hands together and picked up the piece of paper. She cleared her throat and looked around, then back to the paper. "It's the story of four regular city girls. They drink a lot. Because of that, they do a lot of stupid shit. One night, the stupid thing in question consists of ordering pizza and kidnapping the delivery boy, who they tie up and lock in the closet with John Mayer." She put the paper down. "That's all I've got."

"That's awesome! Let's do it," said Kat, leaning over to grab the phone from the floor.

"Do what?" asked Maddy.

"Kidnap a pizza boy!" Kat laughed as she dialled. "Hello, I'd like to order two—two? No, three large vegetarian pizzas."

"Eww, vegetarian?" Bee scrunched up her face.

Lo was nodding vigorously. "Yeah, what?"

"Shut up! I speak for the animals! Sorry, yes? Can you send us your cutest delivery guy, please? Two hundred, Cool Street. No, I'm not kidding. Number forty-five. Thanks." Kat sat back. The girls all shook their heads. "Well, aren't you hungry?"

They laughed, fell back onto the sofas, and poured more drinks. When the buzzer finally rang, Lo hurried to the intercom. "Yes?"

"Pizza delivery."

She let him up. They all looked at each other with a twinkle of crazy in their eyes.

"Maddy, what's the plan?" asked Kat.

"What do you mean *what's the plan*? There is no plan! I just jotted it down as an idea for a story, you crazy bitch. I love you."

"Exactly. Somewhere in you, the full story lies, awaiting its, err, *unfoldment*. Anyway, just let it out."

"Let it out? Well, I guess I would have the girls lure him inside with their fluttery eyelashes and the promise of beer. Then they'd tie him up."

There was a knock at the door.

"Okay, get ready!"

"This is absolutely nuts," said Lo, opening the door. "Hello!"

The delivery boy wasn't *that* cute, but he would do. Lo took the boxes from him.

"It comes to thirty-two fifty," he said, glancing past Lo, stiffening at the sight of the other three girls leering from the doorway, coy smiles on their lips. "Um, there was a special … tonight only."

Lo popped back out of the kitchen with the money and handed it to him. "Keep the change. Hey, um, what's your name?"

"My name?"

"Ya, your name," Kat said, stepping past Lo. "You got a name?"

"It's Jake."

Closing the gap, Bee took his hand and put a beer in it, letting go only once the confused boy had tightened his fingers around it. She grabbed his shirt collar and pulled him into the apartment.

"Come," she said, "come have a beer before you continue your shift."

They made it to the couches, Bee guiding him by the shoulders, Maddy caressing his arm, and Kat walking backwards before him, unbuttoning her blouse.

"Whoa. I'm sorry, I really have to get back to work."

He ducked out from under the many hands but, before he could make it to the door, Maddy had grabbed a hold of his wrist, halting his momentum.

"Oh, but you don't know what you'd be missing, Jakey boy," she said, pulling him towards her. Bee now clutched his other arm.

He wriggled harder. "I gotta go," he said with resolve and, just as he had slipped out of their grips, Lo struck him in the back of the head with a cast iron frying pan.

He fell into a heap on the floor.

Bee stared, mouth hanging open. "What the fuck, Lo?!"

The pan fell from Lo's grip. "I'm sorry!" she managed. "I panicked! I just wanted to give him a little knock, you know, to slow him down."

Kat glanced down at the boy's still body and cackled. "You slowed him down all right!"

"It's not funny," said Bee, crouching over the pile of Jake. She put her fingers to his jugular, then inspected the skin of his scalp where he was struck. "No blood under the skin. Thank God."

Kat nodded, impressed with her friend's nursing skills.

"I'm sorry, I'm so drunk." Lo rubbed her head.

"Well, you want to know what I think?" said Kat, swigging from her bottle of wine.

The girls grunted.

"I think we got ourselves a kidnapped pizza boy!"

"Shut up."

"You're insane."

"Cool." That was Maddy. A little piece of paper with scribbles on it and, just as easily, there, on their blue carpet, was one of her characters, ready to be bound and stashed into the closet with John Mayer.

"Isn't it magical? I write this little idea and *poof!* We have ourselves a pizza boy—named Jake no less!" She looked at her whiskey bottle as if it was a long-lost friend and gave it a good, long drink.

"By *poof* you mean *bam?*" said Kat.

Lo rubbed her head again, as if she'd been the one who'd been beaten with cookware.

Kat plucked the pan from the floor and held it up to the light. "No blood here either." She nodded and left for the kitchen. Lo sat down beside Jake.

"I wonder how long he'll be out."

"I don't know, but we should tie him up now. He's going to freak out when he wakes up," said Maddy, disappearing into her bedroom and reappearing with rope. She kneeled at Jake's feet and pulled his legs straight. "Help me out, Lo."

"I don't know what to do."

Maddy passed the end of the rope to her. "Here, you hold this, I'll wrap him up."

"Wrap him? Tie his hands together and then his ankles, you twit," said Kat.

"Like a pig?"

"Like a pig."

Kat handed her a fillet knife she had brought back from the kitchen.

"We have scissors, you know," said Maddy.

"Yes, but this is so much more badass."

"Don't forget his mouth!" said Bee from the couch, clutching a fresh drink and causally swinging one foot, legs crossed. "Just like in the movies."

"Of course, Bee baby. You're so smart!" said Kat, and dove onto her like a flying squirrel. Meanwhile, Lo got a rag from under the sink and carefully placed it in Jake's mouth.

"That's disgusting, Lo; we clean the bathroom with that," said Maddy.

"Oh." Lo pulled the rag out of Jake's mouth and went to get a washcloth instead. They stuffed it in, Lo pulling on his tongue so that it wouldn't get shoved in the back of his throat with the washcloth.

"You're so considerate," Maddy said to her.

Lo smiled, then hiccupped. "Tape?"

Kat squirrelled through the apartment and lobbed a roll at them. With his head wrapped around a few times with packing tape, Jake perfectly looked the part. A perfect hostage.

"Now what?" Maddy looked up at Kat, as if her decision to order the pizza had made her the big cheese.

"It's your story," she replied with a shrug, "you tell me."

Spaghetti Sauce

Tapping a finger to her lip, Maddy thought for a moment before stating the obvious.

"Well, into the closet he goes. I must say, though, I'm a bit disappointed. We hardly had the chance to flutter our eyelashes." She looked at Jake lying peacefully before her. "He looks so sweet. I'm sure he'd have loved to have been properly wooed. Oh well."

She grabbed him under the arms while Kat grabbed his legs. Staggering and cursing, and with Bee and Lo pulling on the hem of his jeans and his tee-shirt, they heaved—but Jake's butt still dragged across the carpet the whole way.

Once the unconscious boy was plopped in front of the broom closet, the girls paused, glancing at one another.

"How are we going to get him in?" Bee said.

Kat stared down at Jake's now-pale face. "Legs first, I say."

"I think we should sit him in there. He'll be more comfortable," said Lo.

"There'll be no room for his legs if he goes in sitting. We'd have to fold him in half."

"He won't fit folded in half."

"He needs to be standing."

They looked at the body and huffed.

"Okay guys, my story. His head goes in the closet with John, and his body lies out here on the carpet, where we can keep an eye on him. You know, in case he wakes up." Maddy grabbed Jake's arms and tugged, not waiting for the others' approval.

Lo fetched a pillow and placed it at the bottom of the closet under Jake's head, the washcloth still secure in his mouth. The girls exhaled loudly, content with their work. They went back to the couches and took up their drinks.

"What happens next?" asked Bee.

"Well, John Mayer has to be singing to make this part complete. But, since John Mayer's not *actually* in the closet, it's not as fun."

Lo was silent for a moment, face puckered up in thought. Finally, she grinned. "Let's put the speakers in with Jake! Just like your story says."

"On it!" said Kat. "Crank it up!"

And so it was that the girls sang along and drank like rowdy pirates, forgetting their plunder. A good four songs had passed before Kat noticed that Jake had wiggled his head out of the broom closet.

"Guys, guys!" she cried, pouncing from the sofa. "How long has Jake been awake?"

Jake stopped still, tucking in his chin and looking up with round, panicked eyes.

"Whoops!" said Bee.

"What comes next, Maddy?" asked Lo, enthused.

Maddy turned to her, cocking an eyebrow— normally Lo was so nervous—and stood up to assess the situation. She grabbed the remote and turned down the music.

"Are you okay?" she yelled at Jake.

He shook his head hard and stopped abruptly, grimacing in pain.

"You're not? Are you hurt?"

He closed his eyes, took a deep breath, and shook his head again, this time with a little less heart.

"Well, that's good, considering you got knocked out, huh?" said Kat, making Lo blush.

"I'm sorry if I hurt you, Jake," Lo said. "I panicked a little. See we wanted to …"

"Shush!" said Kat. "We need to maintain mystery. Jake doesn't know anything about us except that we like vegetarian pizza."

"Except that we don't like vegetarian pizza," said Bee. Behind her, Maddy pretended to puke.

"Even better. Ha. We don't even *like* vegetarian pizza!" said Kat.

"Kat, *you* ordered it," said Bee.

"Shhhhhh. Don't say my name!"

"Oh, great idea!" said Lo, clapping her hands. "My alias will be Gwendolyn."

Maddy laughed. "Wow, how long have you had that name in your pocket, just waiting to be used?".

"She uses it every Sunday afternoon, on her dates with Ca—"

Lo glared at her.

"Callum," Bee finished. "You know, brown hair, green skin, from Mars."

Kat was making smooching faces. "Kinky!"

"Okay, well, me too," said Bee. "My name is going to be *Apple.*"

"Good one," said Lo.

They all nodded. Never ones to be left out, Maddy chose "Kitty" and Kat chose "Wiggles."

"Okay, Kitty. What comes next then?" said Bee.

"Wait, he knows where we live. Do you remember our address?" Maddy asked Jake. He shook his head over and over. "Where's the paper with our address on it?"

Jake shrugged and then looked around as best he could. When he spotted his messenger bag, he nodded towards it. Bee rifled through its pockets until she found their order.

"Good," said Maddy, giving Bee a high-five. "Now, my story states that we were supposed to woo you. You didn't really let us do that, so my friend Gwendolyn here had to smack you across the head. Last-minute changes happen when you let creativity take the reins."

Jake listened, blinking as his eyes darted around the room, obviously staking the place out.

"Oh no you don't!" said Maddy. She ran to her room and came back with a strip of black cloth, which she pulled over his eyes and tied at the back of his head. She kneeled beside him.

"Now you're going to have to answer with nods. Okay?"

Jake nodded.

"What's your favourite food?" Maddy asked.

Jake stayed quiet and immobile.

She lightly slapped at his cheek. "I said, what's your favourite food?"

This time he answered—something intelligible through the washcloth.

"Okay," she said, sighing. "Promise not to scream?"

When he nodded, Maddy cut the tape and pulled the cloth out. Jake smacked his tongue, his mouth dry.

"Here." Lo lifted Jake's head and tipped a beer bottle to his lips.

"Thanks," he said. "I like spaghetti. Though I think I'm going to puke."

"Spaghetti," they all repeated, not overly impressed but not disappointed either.

"Girls, let's make the boy some noodles!"

And so Lo put Jake's head back down and they all went into the kitchen, bringing John Mayer with them.

The phone rang, and the girls wouldn't have heard it if Jake hadn't called out. Maddy took the call from the bathroom with the door closed, in case he yelled.

"She's so smart!" Lo exclaimed, marvelling at Maddy's quick thinking. "What a great criminal she'd be."

It was the pizzeria. They wanted to know if they had received their order. They were trying to figure out where their delivery boy was, as he should have been back. Yes, they had gotten their pizza and it was delicious thank you, the delivery boy had left right after getting paid. Sorry you lost him.

"I just lied to the pizza boss," said Maddy, emerging from the bathroom. "He didn't suspect a thing."

"Of course not. Since when do drunk girls kidnap delivery boys?" said Bee.

"Since now, obviously! We are spear-headers, girls," said Kat. "Pioneers."

It was half-past midnight by the time the spaghetti was ladled into plates with a side of cold pizza. They cleared the coffee table and set up there. Kat and Maddy dragged Jake over and sat him upright on the couch.

"Wouldn't you rather untie my legs?" Jake said, the black cloth still over his eyes.

"But then you could run away," said Maddy.

"Or *kick* us," suggested Lo.

The girls nodded sagely. Drinks replenished, they dove into the food, humming with delight. "Are you hungry, Jake?" Bee said. "We made the spaghetti especially for you. Can you smell it?"

"Um, yeah. It smells pretty good."

"Oooh, 'pretty good!'" she said in a sing-song voice, raising her hands to the others.

Maddy, smirking, twisted a fork in the plate set in front of Jake and brought the nest of pasta to his mouth.

"Coo-coo, open up!" she said. He did, albeit reluctantly, and she pushed the food into his mouth. His teeth came down on the fork and she pulled it out slowly.

"It's good," he said, chewing. "And I should know, our restaurant makes good Italian."

His mouth still busy with the pasta, Maddy leaned in and kissed him on the lips, tasting the sauce. Jake swallowed fast, hurrying to kiss her back. He smiled, licking his lips.

"What? Ma—Kitty! You saucy feline!" said Bee in a sudden British accent. Kat *ooh*-ed, but Lo pursed her lips.

"You don't know where that mouth has been."

"I was just checking," said Maddy.

Bee coughed. "Checking for what?"

"What the next part of my story will be."

Jake squirmed in his seat, his smile gone.

"He tastes a little young," said Maddy.

"Virgin young?" asked Kat. They all looked at Jake.

After a moment, he shook his head.

"Good to know. Hey, wait a minute. Jake, you wouldn't be having fun, would you?"

Jake didn't respond. Finally, he moved his head up and down, slowly.

"Dude, there's no more washcloth in your mouth, you can speak civilized now."

"Oh, civilized like you, keeping me tied up?" he said.

"Burn!"

"Sarcastic little tyke," said Maddy, tapping her finger to her lips again.

As the pizza slowly disappeared, each of them took turns feeding Jake. In the end, they all tasted the sauce from his mouth—even Lo.

"I can't believe I just did that," she said, wiping her tongue with a paper towel.

It was getting rather late, but the girls didn't want to go to sleep just yet. They had Jake to take care of and a story to finish. It was two in the morning when Kat suggested some uppers.

"How are they with alcohol?" asked Bee.

"Divine," said Kat.

"I don't think that's a good idea," said Lo, rubbing her tired eyes.

Maddy, who was sitting with her legs over Jake's lap and combing his hair with her fingers, tsk-ed her. "When they wear out, we're done. Jake is free and we sleep until Monday. What do you think, Jake?"

"What are you going to tell people, Jake?" asked Bee.

Jake licked his lips and smiled.

"That I got kidnapped by random girls off the street and that I'm not pressing charges. As long as you don't hurt me, that is."

"Sounds like a mighty fine answer," said Kat, dropping the pills into the open hands around the table. Maddy nudged her extra two past Jake's lips.

"Um," said Jake, after he'd swallowed.

"Yes, Jake?"

"I need to … *go to the loo.*"

"Uh-oh," said Lo.

"I got it." Maddy got up, barely catching herself from toppling backwards. "Okay, buddy, you need to help yourself a little here."

His hands reached out and Maddy pulled him to his feet. He hopped, led by the wrist-rope, all the way to the bathroom. They both entered and, a while later, re-emerged, Jake's face flushed red, to find John Mayer awake, Lo dancing, and Bee tidying up. Kat had vanished.

"That was long! Did he take a dump?" asked Bee.

"No!" said Maddy. "Gross. He just needed a little help aiming."

Bee rolled her eyes and chuckled, and Lo stopped dancing.

"Did you wash your hands?" she asked.

"Yes, Mommy. Just before we made out."

"What?" said Bee. Lo shook her head and kept dancing, using her beer bottle to play air-guitar between sips.

At once, Kat reappeared, jumping from her room with a dress in her hands.

"Let's dress him up!"

Just a Tinkle

"Oh là là!"

Lo whistled slowly as she pulled Jake's pants down his legs.

"Oh no, his hands," said Kat.

She was right: though he was down to his underwear and blindfold, the young man's t-shirt still dangled from his bound wrists.

The girls looked to Maddy, the official orchestrator of the whole fiasco.

"We unbind him."

"Aye."

"Then rebind him."

"Aye."

"We work quickly."

"Aye, aye!"

Pulls and tugs, cutting and wrapping; the boy was held in place through each of the steps of his makeover.

"Hold his hands, bucko!"

"Arms through the holes!"

"Heave ho, scallywags!"

"No prey, no pay, hearties!"

"Belay the rope!"

Jake didn't resist; his limbs flung left and right like a rag doll's.

"Pirates," he mumbled. "Of course."

"Sink me!" said Kat. "The lad's getting mouthy!"

"Shall we hang 'im from the yardarm, sir?" asked Bee.

"How 'bout good ol' floggin'. Across the arse," said Kat.

"That's a wee bit dir'y," said Lo.

"Lassies, I've got it. Our little knave will sing us a love song," said Maddy.

"Well, that's not much of a punishment," said Lo, humphing.

"It depends. He could be shy. It could be painful for him."

"It might be painful for *us*," added Kat.

"Oh, and Jake, do include each of us swashbucklers in your song. And you may say *pleasant* things only. It is a love song, after all," concluded Maddy.

The girls stepped back, admiring their work. A lovely knee-length red summer dress, speckled with white polka dots and garnished with a big bow at the bottom crest of the neckline—and curve-less Jake filled it poorly.

They pushed him to the ground by the shoulders and sat in a semi-circle in front of him, drinks at the ready.

"Wait! John Mayer," said Lo, who ran to get the remote to shut him up proper. She detoured through the kitchen and came back with a rolling pin. Having rejoined the audience, she leaned forward and poked Jake in the belly. "Sing! You crossdressing rapscallion!"

Jake took a deep breath and cleared his throat. He began with a few simple *oohs* and then broke off into beautiful, melodic flourishes. The girls roared.

"We're the luckiest girls in the world," said Lo, raising her rolling pin to the sky.

Jake ad-libbed a little longer and finally began adding words to his song. It went something like this:

"Gwendolyn, you're sweet, so sweet, but you poke me in the ribs;

It hurts, but not as bad as my ego, because someone held my wee-wee as I peed oh;

It was you, Kitty, you brave thing, storytelling your tongue past my lips;

I'm glad I didn't get spanked, I think it's clear, Wiggles you're a minx, a minx;

Apple, you seem to have it together, I'd love to see what your ma and pa gave ya;

Apple, are you as green as a bean, or red, as I dream your cheeks ought to be;

Your cheeks so red when I kiss them to sleep."

The girls cheered and rewarded him with a sip from each of their drinks.

"That was lovely!" said Bee, blushing.

"So perceptive for someone who can't see a thing," said Maddy.

"He's even better than John!" Lo shrieked.

"What now? I'm feeling revitalized," said Bee, looking to Maddy for a solution.

"We could take a walk?"

"With *him?*"

"Well, we can't leave him. What if he needs to pee again? I don't want to have to clean that up."

"So true," said Lo.

"Let's take a walk in the building," suggested Bee.

"That's a great idea," said Maddy. "We'll have to untie Jake's ankles. What do you say, Jake? Are you going to run away?"

"Of course not, this is the most fun I've ever had."

"He's being sarcastic again," said Kat.

"We're serious, Jake, we can tie you to the toilet bowl, or you can come with us and not run away." Maddy looked at the girls for their approval.

"I won't run away," said Jake.

"Good enough."

"Do we take off his blindfold?" asked Lo.

"No way. If he sees our faces, he could identify us in a line-up. We could do some serious jail time."

"He saw us when he first arrived," said Kat.

"Just a little." Maddy shrugged. "You wouldn't be able to identify us, would you, Jake?"

"Of course not," he said. "You are completely forgettable."

"Hey!" exclaimed Kat, offended.

Lo snorted. "Jail time? It's not like we killed him or anything."

Jake's lips tightened into a line. As much as he was having fun, he realized that he didn't know how far these girls would let their mischief go. Were they just drunk, or really nuts?

"All right. So, what time is it?" asked Maddy as she cut the rope from Jake's ankles.

"Almost three," said Kat.

"Okay, guys, we're going to do this quietly, because we can't have witnesses. Jake might be okay with our crime, but others surely will not be." Maddy's serious eyes looked for a glimmer of understanding from each of them. "Lo?"

"Yes, Mommy," she said, sticking her tongue out.

They clambered to their feet and made it out the door in a buzzing cloud of giggles. Leaving the door unlocked behind them, they headed down the hall.

"Oh, we should go see Lily," said Lo.

"Have you not been listening? This is a covert operation!" said Maddy.

A few doors down, Lo knocked on Lily's door. Maddy rolled her eyes at the insubordinate child she had for a friend. The others groaned.

Just when they were about to make a run for it, Lily opened the door. She sparkled in a black sequinned dress.

"Ooh," Lo said, "You've been out!"

"Yeah, I just got back. What's this all about?" Lily didn't smile, but nodded to the gang behind Lo.

"Oh, we're going for a walk through the building. You wanna come with?"

"Covert, Gwendolyn!" repeated Maddy under her breath.

"Sure." Lily stepped out and closed the door behind her. "What's with the fake name?"

"Oh yes, that's right. Gwen." Lo pointed to herself. "Wiggles, Apple, and Kitty. Please use those."

"And her? I mean, them?" said Lily, pointing at Jake.

"Him?" said Lo. "That's, um, Beau. Curious Beau."

Maddy put her hand on Jake's shoulder. "Curious Beau sings really well. Better than John Mayer. Sing for our friend, Curious Beau!"

And Jake began singing Elvis's 'Can't Help Falling in Love,' all the way down the hall and into the stairwell, where the acoustics where excellent. They went down a level. The girls each took turns poking Jake in the ribs with the rolling pin so that he'd keep it down, as he always got carried away every time the chorus came around.

They walked down the carpeted corridor, remnants of smells narrating stories of hamburger dinner, kitty litter, and reefer.

"There really is no filter between the inside smells and the outside world is there?" asked Bee.

"I wonder what our place smells like from the outside," said Lo.

"Probably smells like four hot chicks," said Kat.

"And what is that supposed to smell like?"

Kat gently bopped her head to the Elvis song while she considered this.

"Well," she said at last, "chocolate, Chanel, and fresh bread. Obviously."

Jake smiled widely as he continued to sing his song in a flawless loop, Lo leading him by the wrist-rope.

Down another floor.

"Hey." A young man's voice was heard. With him were two other men, and all three walked straight towards the wandering troubadours. "You're the girls that threw the bra! Hey, you wanna come party with us? We're gonna be up *all* night." The guys chuckled, looking the girls up and down, faces twisted into hungry grins. No one seemed to notice the blindfolded crossdresser.

Lo gave a quick sniff, eyes dispassionately scanning these new creatures. They smelled of the bad kind of drunk—all violence and repressed lust. While Jake kept softly singing, the rolling pin musical-chaired its way from one pair of hands to the next, until Lo had it clutched in both hands. She brandished it like the swashbuckler she was.

"We're not interested!" she cawed.

The men's eyes grew wide. "Whoa, crazy lady," the first guy said, opening the door behind him. They backed up and disappeared inside.

"Careful who you call a lady!"

"Number twenty-three. We'll know where to play Nicky Nicky Nine Doors at five in the morning," said Maddy, shaking her fist at the door.

"Ding Dong Ditch, bitch," said Bee, mimicking Maddy as she passed.

"Knock Down Ginger, stinker," said Lo, still brandishing her baking weapon.

Lily, meanwhile, quietly flipped her middle finger.

Jake still hadn't stopped singing. He kept serenading them at modest volume all the way back to Lily's pad, where she bid them adieu and watched them march off to number forty-five.

"What the hell?" said Bee as she stepped in, leaving indents in the wet sponge the carpet had become. She sloshed around, her hands up in the air. "What the hell?"

"Holy shit!" said Maddy, stumbling in next with Jake hanging off her arm. The place had flooded.

"It's the toilet." Lo tossed the rolling pin to the side and poked an accusatory finger, which seemed even more dangerous than the pin, into their abductee's chest. "Jake, did you *poop?*"

"No! I swear! It was just a tinkle."

"Dammit." They each took their turn with the word as they paced the waterlogged apartment. Maddy ran to the bathroom and got down on her knees.

"There's water spurting out of this pipe!" she called out behind her. "Give me something!"

Handed a wrench, she grunted as she tried to fit it around the pipe, fiddling until she finally yanked with a mighty yell, her hand flying backward with the tool and knocking Jake right between the eyes. He crashed to the floor like a felled tree.

Maddy turned and saw him flat on his back. "What the fuck? Why was he standing so close?"

"Get him out of the poo water!" shouted Lo.

Maddy crawled out, a peacock tail of water still spurting behind her, and Bee waded past her, found the knob to the water supply, and turned it off.

"You could have told us you were a plumber," said Maddy.

They all kneeled around Jake. He had blood on his forehead. Maddy finally removed the blindfold.

"Aw, I forgot he had blue eyes," said Lo, pulling up his eyelids.

Maddy shook him, his body sagging back and forth. She suddenly felt very sober. "Let's bring him to the couch."

Dragging him across the wet carpet, they heaved on three and dropped him among the cushions. Side by side, they looked down at him.

"Someone ought to check his pulse," said Bee.

"Lo should do it," said Kat.

"Why?" said Lo.

"Because you're the nursey one."

"Whatever. I think Maddy should check."

"Why?" said Maddy.

"Because it's your story. You did this."

Maddy pouted. "Don't do that. We all did this. You egged me on, if anything."

"Yes, that's a low blow from you, Lo," said Kat. "You fucking knocked him out with the frying pan first."

Lo stared at her for a long moment, but finally sighed. "You're right. I did," she said, massaging her temple. "And I'm sorry. I'm just freaking out a little. I don't want to be the one to check. I don't think I'd be able to keep my head if he were dead."

"I don't think any of us would," said Bee.

"Oh, move over, you wimps." Just as Kat bent down to check Jake's jugular, the walls trembled, the ground shook, and objects rattled, fell, and shattered in the kitchen. The girls hung onto each other until, at last, the earth's belly-grumble passed.

"What was that?" asked Lo.

"An earthquake," Maddy whispered.

Bee stepped out onto the balcony. The world was asleep. It was four in the morning and all the club hoppers had gone home. The streets were vacant but well lit; power hadn't gone out. No noise came from the lower levels, no screams from residents caught beneath their toppled china cabinets. A streak in the night sky caught Bee's eye: a thick and billowy contrail, light grey against the dark vault of heaven. It started as a fine point, stretching too far to discern its origin, and drew a widening channel towards their building, disappearing above it.

"Girls," said Bee quietly, making her way back to the couches. "There's a huge trail of smoke in the sky, leading right to us. I bet that's what shook the building." She paused as if waiting for the others to piece it together. "Something's crashed on our roof."

"That's ridiculous," said Maddy, scoffing.

"Go see for yourself."

They went to the balcony, Bee staying behind to tentatively check Jake's pulse. Untying the rope from his wrists, chafed red bands were exposed. She caressed them tenderly and placed her hand on his cheek.

"Poor Jake," she murmured.

"What an idiot," said Bee when the girls returned. "Look at the mess he let himself get into. Maddy, I think we know now. Stories are dangerous."

"He's not dead, is he?" asked Lo.

Bee shook her head.

Maddy dropped herself into the couch. "Bee, if I ever see you burning a book, I can't be your friend anymore." She gave a small smile. "Even if we *are* blood sisters. But look, you can burn my little note if it makes you feel better. Although, it's too late—we've played out what was written on it."

"I don't want to burn anything."

"Good. Because the story isn't over. There's nothing to burn but my mind." She stood up suddenly, apparently refreshed. "Come on. We're going to the roof."

"What about Jake?" asked Bee.

"Leave him. He's not going anywhere," assured the storyteller.

As they made their way out, the girls stomped on the wet carpet, trying to send water splashing as far as they could.

At the top of the stairwell was a metal door that opened into a small shack, and the small shack's door onto the roof. Both were unlocked. Hand on the doorknob, Maddy hesitated.

"Come on," Kat whispered. "Open the door. It's dark in here and there might be rats."

"There are no rats in this building," answered Lo's hushed voice from somewhere in the shadows.

"How do you know?"

"Because, cats."

"There are no cats in the building."

"Sure there are. I've seen 'em. And you know cats: they don't happily endure lower life forms. Even higher lifeforms. Heck, I bet they'd take over the world if they could."

A small gust of wind caught the door as Maddy pushed it open, swinging it wide against the shack's shell with a clang. The four girls cringed, still wanting to be inconspicuous though they knew not why, and relaxed when the silence had reinstated itself. They stepped out and looked around.

The night was well lit, a glow from the city below rising like haze above the sea of buzzing street lamps and flickering neon signs. Small grey rocks covered the roof's shingles, crunching softly beneath their feet. Metal tubes of various sizes protruded here and there, taut black wires running between them. Further back, a lump of metal the size of a two-seater car produced a wide artery of smoke.

"I don't like the looks of that." Lo's hand reached for Kat's and held it tight.

"It's probably a meteorite or something," said Bee.

"It looks like an electric car," said Maddy.

"Cars don't fly," said Kat.

"Hoooly shit, guys," whined Lo.

"It's okay, baby Lo, we're fine. Maybe it's a secret government thing. A drone maybe."

"What if it's a UFO?" Maddy said, gesturing wildly. "If it is, whatever drove it must be dead. Look at that smoke."

Kat squeezed Lo's hand. Bee and Maddy, not wanting to be left out, grasped for free hands. Linked together, they took a few steps closer.

"What if they aren't dead?" Lo let out a worried moan. "What if they want to kill us?" She began to shake.

"Panicking will get us nowhere," said Maddy, her voice firm, as they pussyfooted over the crunching rocks.

They were only ten feet away now, none ready to close the gap between them and whatever the hunk of metal was—and, more importantly, whatever it might contain. They would have dragged out the processional even further had the skies not cracked with thunder and began pummelling them with rain.

"Abort!" yelled Kat.

"Look!" called out Lo, pointing to the electric car lookalike. The rain had put out the fire and the smoke had begun to fade, caught in the strong wind. It still looked like an electric car, but one with black airplane wings, hardly noticeable against the dark sky behind.

The girls took a few more steps, their hands held like hat brims to protect their peering eyes from the rain.

"Something's moving inside," Kat said, her voice barely above a whisper. With a trembling hand, she reached out ….

"No, Kat!"

"It's fine, Lo." Shaking her head, Kat cupped her hands to the glass and peeked. She froze.

"Kat? What is it?" Maddy said.

"Oh. My. God."

Her hands quickly searched for a door, sliding up and down and along the sides until she found a groove.

"Got it." She dug her fingers in.

"What are you doing? Don't open it!" said Lo, nailed in place, fists clenched in her hair.

Kat wrenched open the door and fell to her knees before the dark hole. She held out her hands as if awaiting the embrace of a child.

A tiny limb felt around. A paw—perfect, fragile, covered in white fur. It found Kat's hands and, unsteadily, stepped out into them.

"Oh my god," said Bee.

"I can't believe this," said Maddy.

"It's a little kitten!" squealed Lo, joining Kat in the doorway, the airplane wing providing shelter from the rain. "Oh my goodness, there are at least a dozen in here!" She reached out her hands and let a kitten crawl into her arms.

Bee followed, awe pulling her down to her knees. But Maddy stayed on her feet, squinting eyes peering through the fogged-up window, the rain still beating down around her.

"How can there be kittens in here? Kittens can't drive!"

"Oh Maddy, does it matter? Look at them. The poor babies must be *traumatized*." Lo pulled the kitten to her chest and rocked it.

"There might be something else in there," Maddy said, ignoring her. Gently, she pushed the others aside and poked her head inside the craft. Her girlfriends were clearly not considering the possibility of an aggressive alien leader with a driver's license.

But there was nothing else, from what she could see in the dark, except for more kittens and a ridiculous number of colourful, crinkly candy wrappers. She picked up one up. The label read: *Space Candy*.

"I knew it! They're space cats! Girls, put them back!" Maddy recoiled sharply, stepping back into the rain that had mellowed to a drizzle.

"Are you nuts?" said Bee, accepting several more kittens from Kat. "We are *so* taking them home."

"You're the ones who are nuts!" Maddy twirled her finger at her temples and pointed to the little kittens. "These aren't normal cats! They can *drive!* Who knows what else they can do!"

"It could be a self-driving vehicle, you know. And there's no proof they're from space. Do you know how ridiculous that sounds? I bet they were just on a trip from, you know, *somewhere else*, and the craft glitched," said Bee.

"Maybe they're from Arizona," said Lo.

"Kat?" said Maddy, thinking—hoping—she'd get a reasonable response.

"Sorry, Maddy. Three against one."

The hems of their shirts became little hammocks, and the kittens were plopped in, four per sac.

"There's one left," said Lo. "You have to carry him, Maddy."

Maddy considered this. It was a dangerous thing, bringing these crash-landed kittens into their home.

They were practically strays. They could be carrying space fleas. Or Arizona fleas.

Little furry heads poked out of her friends' tenderly folded shirts and looked up at her. They seemed harmless, but were too cute to be trusted. Maddy knew this. The girls turned to her and, with the same affection-hungry eyes as the kittens they cradled, pleaded without saying a word.

Paws curled over the edge of the hole-shaped doorway; the last kitty, a particularly round one, trying in vain to get out.

"You're stuck huh?" said Maddy, looking down at it. It was a splotchy black-and-white kitty, with a little "M" on his forehead marking him as a tabby. It looked up at her, apparently listening. They stared at each other for some time. Finally, she sighed. "You guys would have been in trouble up here if it weren't for us. Or, at least, *you* would have, since your friends over there obviously used you as a stepping stool. Still, they'd have been stuck on this roof. That's worse than being stuck in a tree. At least in a tree, people can see you as they walk by. There's a chance of rescue. But not a roof. Remember that. We helped you. So don't kill us with your laser eyes —shit, I bet you have laser eyes."

Maddy picked up the cat, her heart melting the second its warm little body was in her hands. She held it up near her face, touching her nose to his. "Don't gimme no fleas," she said in a pouty baby voice. And back inside they went, down to number forty-five with their precious cargo.

The girls, twittering like birds, walked into their apartment. The carpet was still very much soaked.

"I'd forgotten about this mess," said Kat, putting her kittens down. She pulled out all the towels they had and spread them across the floor. Meanwhile, Lo went into the kitchen and came back with a bowl. The cats released from their shirt-hammocks, they crowded around it, their faces soon covered in milk. Maddy let hers go last.

"That black-and-white one's mine," she said.

"They're all ours, Maddy," said Lo. "No need to be possessive. We have so many."

"Maybe we should give some away?" said Bee.

"No!" The other three answered in unison.

"You're right. Let's keep them all."

They watched as the kittens drank from the bowl, a few allowing themselves to be left out of the cramped circle before forcing their way back to the rim. The little meows and purrs were calming, and the girls sat on the couches, utterly relaxed.

"I think I'm about ready for sleep," said Maddy. The sky was beginning to lighten outside.

"You go ahead," said Lo. "I'm going to make a bed for these guys and some sort of litter box. You think they'll pee on Cheerios? Or would Rice Krispies be better?"

"Definitely Rice Krispies," said Bee.

Maddy frowned. Something was off. Cocking her head as she looked around, she suddenly realized what it was. "Fuck. *Fuck!*"

"What is it?" said Kat.

"Jake! He's gone!"

The girls mumbled their worried complaints as they glanced around, none of them getting up—until Kat pulled herself upright and went to check the rooms.

"Do you think he'll tell on us?" asked Lo.

"I don't know," said Maddy. "Maybe. We did knock him out twice."

"But he sang for us," said Lo, reaching down to pet a few kittens.

"Should we go looking for him?" asked Bee.

"Nah," was Maddy's reply.

"Well, he didn't take any jewelry or nothing," said Kat, emerging from Maddy's bedroom. "And his clothes are still here. That means he's walking around in my polka dot dress. Dammit. I liked that dress."

One after the other, they disappeared into their rooms—all except for Lo, who put her legs up on the couch and watched the kittens finish off the milk. Then, forgetting the bed and litter box, she fell into a sweet sleep.

Clean as a Whistle

At around ten o'clock, life began to stir. The sun had coated the apartment with gold.

"Good morning, Bee," said Kat as she joined her at the tiny kitchen table, a steaming coffee clutched in both hands.

"Shh, Lo is still sleeping."

"What the hell happened?" they heard Maddy yell. Glancing at one another, they hurried into the living room, finding a shocked Lo sitting upright, blinking back sleep. On the other couch were the cats. But there were no longer thirteen; they were at least double that.

"Nooo! We've got gremlin cats! We fed them after midnight and they multiplied!" screamed Maddy. She turned to the black-and-white one she had admonished and befriended the night before and pointed her finger at it. "You! We had a deal! No funny stuff!"

It meowed as if in apology, and all the other kittens echoed its cry.

"Shhh, shhhh kitties." Lo tip-toed over, followed by the two others, and knelt in front of the couch. They caressed and kissed them.

"You sentimental fools! Focus!" yelled Maddy. "Where in the world did the extra cats come from?"

Bee held up a fleshy tube attached to some dark, bloody lump. "I think one of them forgot to eat this. Aren't animals supposed to eat this?"

"What the hell is that?" asked Maddy.

"It's an umbilical cord—and a placenta, I think."

Kat and Bee whooped.

"They copulated! The little rascals!" said Kat, slapping her knee like some old timey grandpa.

"But they're just kittens," said Maddy.

"They're very mature for their age," said Lo.

There wasn't any time to waste—not with all those mouths to feed. Off to the store they went, leaving only Lo behind to keep an eye on things. Tidying up and puttering about, she hummed the same John Mayer tune over and over again, looking over every so often to see what their many cats were up to. It was while she was sweeping the kitchen floor that she heard a man's voice in the living room. Choking back a squeal, she clutched her broom, and, holding it high like a battle axe, rushed in to protect her furry babies. But there was no one; no one but the cats. The deep voice boomed again, and she snapped her head towards its source: the black-and-white tabby. It was speaking on the phone.

"Yes, I'm looking for the number of a man called Ray."

Lo's breath caught. She stumbled backwards, bringing several kitchen counter knick-knacks and an empty cup of coffee with her to the floor. The cat carried on its conversation, barely glancing at her, and by the time Lo had picked herself back up, it had hung up.

"You speak English!" she blurted.

The cat looked at her and shook its head.

"But—but you just did!"

It shook its head again, the other twenty or thirty cats joining in.

The door opened. The girls were back with their arms full: a bag of kitty kibble, a litter box, and a family pack of Rice Krispies.

"Guys, these cats aren't normal," said Lo, her face puckered with worry.

"Well yes, I think we figured that one out earlier!" said Maddy, putting down the bag of food by the door. "What did they do now?"

"Well, for one, they speak English."

"English? And not Italian?"

"Also, I don't think we need the litter."

"Why?" said Bee, her face sagging. "We got this really cute teal box."

"Because," continued Lo, "these cats don't go. Don't you think they would have already?"

"Maybe that space candy plugged them up," said Kat. "Give 'em some real food and see what happens."

A scratching noise made them turn. Some of the cats were huddled at the exit, clawing frantically at the door.

"Maybe they do their business outside, like dogs," said Maddy, clearly not averse to the idea. Lo put on her shoes and the girls set out to accompany the army of cats outside, leaving the door unlocked behind them.

The cats flowed down the steps in undulating waves of fluff and rushed through the building's back doors held open for them by Lo.

"Share the responsibility, Lo, or they're gonna like you more," said Maddy.

"What would be so bad about that?" answered Lo as they walked behind the river of cats, the black-and-white one leading from the front.

"Well, obviously they would spare you when their robot brains go haywire from the atmospheric change. Everyone else will be murdered."

"You're silly," said Bee.

"You know they're not from Arizona," said Maddy.

Beneath her, the kittens peered up, mewling with little sounds of admittance.

"And you still want to let them live in our apartment? What if they keep making babies? What if one night they all decide to lie on our faces while we sleep and we just never wake up?"

"They're not going to kill us," said Kat. "Get a grip."

The cats arrived at a patch of grass on the other side of the building's parking lot but walked straight across it. Unlike dogs, they didn't pause to appreciate the smorgasbord of smells and opportunities for relief the green area provided. The girls kept up, following them across a tiny back street and then to a small grassy hill, where they also didn't stop, and down towards another street of houses.

They crossed town using sidewalks and alleyways, sometimes walking through private property so as to avoid undue attention. They moved like a big, hairy amoeba, sticking together, never losing a kitten to the rugged terrain. Finally, the cats stopped in front of a shop, the name *Ray's Clean as a Whistle Dry Cleaner* printed in black letters across a light pink awning. The black-and-white tabby turned and sat, regally facing the girls, and lifted a front paw as if to motion them to stop. They did.

"He's bossy, that one," said Maddy. "Not too smart, though. He would still be in that flying car if I hadn't pulled him out. He was the step-ladder cat."

Lo tsk-ed her. "They speak English; you can't talk bad about them."

"So you say."

"It's true. I heard the bossy one on the phone."

Maddy considered this. "So you're scared of them, then?"

"Absolutely not."

The cats entered the building and the girls waited. Eventually, Bee and Kat hopped over to a shop across the street and brought back some sandwiches for breakfast. They ate in silence.

The sun shifted its position in the sky. Sitting on the curb, Maddy finally jumped up.

"This is stupid. I'm going in."

Standing up one after the other, the girls joined her, a little bell over the sill ringing gently as they opened the door. The cats all turned to look but, seeing who it was, quickly went back to what they were doing.

"Um, one moment, I'll be right with you!" said a man. He was not a tall man, nor was he short. He was medium-sized, with good hair, white and thick. His eyes were dark, sunken half-moons and his round cheekbones were draped with taut, weathered skin.

The cats were all over him. They were clutching his arms, biting, licking, and sucking at his skin. Cats gripped to the front of his shirt, dangling from the hem of his pant pockets, attempting to claw away at the cloth. A cat was perched on each of his shoulders, inspecting the insides of his ears and suckling on his reddened earlobes. On his head sat another. This one pulled on his eyelids with his paws and leaned over his forehead to peer into his eyes. Then, apparently satisfied, he sank his teeth into one of the man's eyebrows and sucked on that.

More cats sat on the counter, facing him, awaiting their turn.

"Can I help you?" said the man after a few minutes, the cats still licking his arms, his cheeks, biting him and making him yelp.

"Well, these are our cats," Maddy said, stepping forward.

"*Your* cats?" said the man, a chuckle escaping between two small squeals of pain. "These aren't anybody's cats."

"You know them?"

"I've dreamt about them," he said. "But this is the first time we've met in flesh. They've come for me."

"And you are?"

"Ray. Nice to meet you." He lifted his arm to a forty-five-degree angle, intending to offer his hand for a shake, but the weight of the cats dangling off it forced him to drop it back down.

Lo stepped forward, her chin jutted out. "Well, that's not going to be good enough, *Ray*. They landed on *our* roof, and they'll be leaving with *us*."

Kat elbowed Lo in the ribs, earning a look of such discontent that Lo—who was supposed to be the gentle, caring one—became hardly recognizable.

"Calm down, mama bear," Kat whispered.

"Yes, they told me about the crash," said Ray matter-of-factly. "Don't worry, they can leave with you. They need a place to stay while they're here."

"What do you mean, 'while they're here?' They're not going to stay?" asked Lo.

"No, Lo," said Maddy. "They're not from here. And they're not from Arizona either. They're goddamn space cats. They should go back where they came from."

One at a time, Ray started plucking the cats off of him. "Well, they won't be able to leave until I give them what they came for."

"And what's that?" asked Maddy.

"I'm afraid I don't know you well enough to share that information. But let's just say if I hadn't been able to provide what they're looking for, they would have deviated their course and crashed into a whole other galaxy. So, enjoy them. They're special."

The black-and-white tabby meowed at him.

"Of course," he told the cat. "I'll do what I can. See you tomorrow."

The animals jumped off the counter.

"Oh and, don't leave them alone in your apartment. Don't lock them in. They'll procreate if you do. It's a defence mechanism. And the gestation period is merely a few hours, so it could get problematic."

"You've just met them and they've already told you about their sex life?" asked Bee.

"They are many, and I am just one. Together—latched on to me as they were—we found common ground. Like a key in the right hole, they unlocked my mind to theirs. Don't look so surprised; I've seen many a weird thing in my life. This is not the weirdest." He smiled, looking thoughtful for a second. "It actually feels the most natural. If ever you have the chance to experience it, I highly suggest it."

"No thanks," said Maddy. She gestured to the cats, indicating it was time to go. As they turned to leave, Ray spoke again.

"Be good to them."

Lo turned around, surprised. "Of course we will!"

"I was talking to the cats," he said, giving the felines an admonishing nod of the head.

The cats followed the girls home. They seemed deep in discussion the entire way, meowing and making funny little sounds cats don't usually make: trills and grunts, and even caws. Forgetting to use the backstreets, they walked right through town, the people they crossed so intrigued by the kitten crowd that they stopped to stare, nudging each other with their elbows and pointing. Cars slowed down, heads popped out of backseat windows. Noticing the traffic jam they were causing, the girls figured it would be better to have the man called Ray come to them next time—if, that is, there was a next time.

Pent Up

Back at the apartment, the cats cuddled on the couch while Bee plucked the soaked towels from the floor and stuck them in the laundry closet in the kitchen.

"We need to call a plumber," she said.

The black-and-white leader shoved a smaller kitty off the couch. Both padded to the bathroom, slamming the door behind them. Another cat sauntered over to the bag of food and sliced it open with a whip of the paw, a deluge of kibbles pouring out onto the carpet.

"Aw come on, that's just impolite," said Maddy, scooping up the food and distributing it into bowls. The cat meowed and the others joined in, swarming like a pack of lions on a fresh kill. In a blur, the food was gone —and the cats took back to the couch, sitting with their bellies out, which they rubbed, whining and spluttering. That was the last time they ate any kitty kibble.

"Girls!" yelled Bee from the bathroom. "The freaking cats fixed the toilet!" She came out holding her hands up and grinning incredulously.

"Well, enjoy their skills while they're here because, apparently, they have somewhere to be." Maddy looked up from the outlet she was bent over, an electric fan held in her arms. "And someone has to stay home with them because these are the horniest cats ever. So, who's it going to be?"

"You," they all said, because Maddy was the only one who could work from home. Bee was a waitress, Kat was a lawyer's secretary, and Lo was a kindergarten teacher. Maddy, though, worked as an analyst for a software company. Every time she tried to explain what she did, the girls quickly forgot, lost in the jargon and the boring details of what sounded like a very square profession.

"You know I'd love to stay," said Lo with a sigh, admiring the bloated cats.

"Fine, I'll work from home with the damn cats. But if they get all up in my hair, I am throwing them off the balcony," said Maddy, opening the patio doors. She peered down at the small people walking by and wondered where they were all going. Maybe they had pets too—normal pets. "I have a feeling they'd land on their feet anyway," she muttered.

Sunday went by without any glitches. Their hangovers met their ends thanks to sporadic power naps and an endless supply of junk food. When Monday rolled around and everyone left for work, Maddy set herself up at the coffee table with her laptop and a fresh cup of coffee.

"Move over," she said to the cats as she sat, forcing them out of the way. Annoyed noises squeaked and beeped out of them.

"That's right. Go cry to your mommies."

Maddy was a bit grumpy about babysitting but, at the same time, she was happy she didn't have to face Jack—she wondered with a wince how he'd taken her phone confession that last Saturday night. It was a shame; he was usually the first thing she thought of when her alarm went off in the morning, the thought of seeing him giving her the motivation she needed to get up and go to work. He was the pep to her step. Who knew how long it would be before she saw him again?

Maddy didn't quite trust how easy it had been to convince her boss to let her work from home. The woman was an unapologetic flirt, and Maddy suspected she had an eye on Jack herself—now, the hunting grounds were clear of unnecessary competition.

"It doesn't matter," Maddy said to the cats, as if they'd been keeping track of her inner ramblings. She opened her laptop and logged in. "Men are just trouble. And I get into enough trouble just with my girls."

Several cats reached up and put their paws on her thighs, as if to comfort her. Maddy looked down at tiny, fluffy appendages, then into the wide eyes of the cats themselves.

"You're a weird bunch, you know that?"

A few uneventful hours passed before there came a knock at the door. Maddy looked at the cats, many of whom were curled up asleep. "Stay here," she told them.

It was Jack. *From-work* Jack.

"What are you doing here?" asked Maddy, her palms instantly sweaty.

"I got a call, from a guy named Tabby."

"What?" Maddy looked at the culprit feline on the couch. The black-and-white tabby waved at her. Maddy scolded him silently, shooting imaginary lasers out of her squinted eyes. The cat remained unfazed and Maddy ushered Jack in. "What did he tell you?"

"Oh, just that you couldn't come into work and that this made you sad because you really wanted to see me. So I suggested coming to you and Tabby said that was a fabulous idea. His words." Jack looked around the apartment. "Holy shit, you have a lot of cats."

"Yes, that's why I can't come to work. They kind of just crashed into our lives and we have to figure out how to adjust."

"We?"

"Me and the girls. I live with three other girls."

"That's right. Hence the party."

Maddy gave a wry smile. "Yeah, we have fun. So, how did you find me?"

"I asked Jimena for your address, but she wouldn't hand it over. She said it was against work policy. So I asked Yoost—you know, from accounting? He said Jimena wouldn't give it to me because she wants me for herself."

"Ha," Maddy said, but didn't smile. She wiped her hands on her hips, inviting him to sit. "Well, that's cool, no? She's an attractive lady."

Jack frowned and followed her to the couches, taking a seat across from her.

"Do you remember calling me on Saturday night?" he asked.

"Do I? Um …" She wanted to say no, sweep the whole thing under the rug. Under the table, a cat dug its claws into her shin. "Ow! Fuck. Yes, I remember."

"Good," said Jack, smiling.

Maddy wiped her hands yet again on her jeans, her nerves wreaking havoc. "Would you excuse me for a minute?"

"Ya, of course." He watched her leave for the bathroom.

When she returned to the living room only moments later, Jack was standing on the coffee table, the cats attacking him from all sides, yowling, hissing, swinging from his body, sharp claws snagged in his clothes. Some had their teeth clamped into him.

"Maddy! Help! Get them off me!" he yelled, trying to pluck the critters away.

Maddy folded her tongue with her fingers and whistled. The cats stopped and turned.

"What the hell, cats? You should be *ashamed* of yourselves! Jack is our guest! Have you no sense of hospitality?"

One by one, the cats dropped and flocked into Lo's bedroom to sulk in peace. Maddy watched them go, then turned to Jack, pleading for forgiveness with her eyes. She offered her hand to help him down. He ignored it and hopped off.

"What a bunch of psychos!" he said, sitting back down.

"You're not leaving?" asked Maddy.

"Hmm? Oh, no. Obviously you know how to control them. Just don't ever leave me alone with them again. I'm lucky I still have my eyes!"

Jack's arms and neck were covered in bloody scratches, much to Maddy's dismay. She promptly fetched some alcohol, swabs, and Band-Aids, and sat close beside him. Their knees touched and her heart sputtered.

"May I?" she asked. He saw the nervousness in her face and nodded, a smile on his lips.

"Well, we got the big ones," she said, putting one last adhesive bandage under his ear. "How do you feel?"

"I feel like I look: like I just got attacked by a bunch of lunatic cats," he said, chuckling.

"You look … perfect."

They stared at each other for too many seconds—and Jack inched closer for a kiss. All shyness dissipated, and Maddy met him halfway with an eagerness that toppled them over. They melted into each other arms, writhing with months of pent-up desire. The cats watched, piled up at the bedroom's threshold, unabashed.

The kissing turned to gentle tasting and, finally, they sat up. Evidently, they knew how to take their time.

"I'll make coffee," said Maddy.

"Thank you, but I have to get back to work. I'm glad I came, though," said Jack, grinning. "You'll have to thank Tabby for me."

Maddy made him promise to visit her again soon, even accounting for the psycho cats. Glowering at the little faces in the bedroom doorway as he walked by, Jack made his way out.

Bee, Kat, and Lo came back from work at the usual time, their arms full of the usual bags of food and alcohol. Perched atop each doming sack were cat toys.

"How was your day, Maddy?" asked Bee. She hopped over and kissed her on the cheek, then wiggled a stuffed mouse on a sick in front of the cats. A few tried to swat it, looking more annoyed than curious.

"It was interesting." Maddy shut her laptop and stretched her legs out, feet on the table. "Jack came to visit earlier."

"What?" said Kat, squeezing her butt into a corner of the couch amid a fresh pool of cats. "You called him?"

"Actually, the cats did. This one." Maddy pointed to the big black-and-white cat with the "M" on his forehead. "He introduced himself to Jack as Tabby. We know you can talk, Tabby. You can stop pretending. Anyway…"

Lo shrieked and jumped out from the kitchen, shaking a newspaper in her hands.

"He's at the Duggers Institute!"

"Who is?" asked Maddy.

Lo placed the paper on the coffee table and tapped her finger repeatedly on the black-and-white picture of Jake, captured sitting in a wheelchair beside a woman in scrubs. The headline read *Pizza Boy Mysteriously Injured, Can No Longer Speak.*

"Front page! He's going to get better and he's going to blab. He will."

"No, he won't," said Kat. "He had fun with us. If anyone sues us, it'll be his family."

"Great," said Lo.

Tabby leapt onto the table then and sat down in the centre. He lifted his little paw authoritatively, like a priest addressing his congregation. Clearly he was the one who drove the space car.

"Stop whining," said the cat in his deep voice. "We will take care of the problem if you let us out of this box you call a home."

The girls stared, all suspicions confirmed.

"Take care of what, exactly? And how?" asked Kat, unfazed, as if conversing with Tabby was a regular, run-of-the-mill thing to be doing.

"We will make sure you do not get into trouble. And then you can stop whining."

"We're not whining!" said Lo.

The cat whipped his head at her, giving her a look they would later dub *The Evil Tabby*.

"Fine," said Maddy. She got up and went to the door. The cats followed her, leaping off the couch and coming out from their various hiding places.

Tabby, at the head of the group, sat down in front of Maddy, who waited with the door open. He gestured with his paw for her to lower herself. She sighed and crouched down. Tabby, apparently unwilling to get up, gestured for her to come closer still and, when she did, he put his paw on her cheek.

"It's going to be okay," he said. And, with that, he rose and the cats pattered out, huddled like a herd of miniature cattle.

Love Bites

"Okay, I think we need to talk about this," said Lo, settling into the couch, hands on her knees.

"About what?" asked Bee.

"About talking cats that fly space cars and give us the evil eye."

"As far as we know, only Tabby can talk," said Bee, as if that lessened the absurdity.

"Well, what can we do?" asked Kat. "We brought them into our home. I think we're stuck with them."

"Do you think if someone else had gone up to the roof, they would be the ones stuck with them instead? Like Lily? Or those oafs from the second floor?" asked Lo.

Kat considered this. "Maybe."

"Do you think that if we asked them to leave, they would?"

"Maybe."

"But do we want that?" asked Maddy, her hand on her cheek, still stunned by Tabby's comforting paw. "You all saw that. I know I've been wishy-washy with these critters, but this is too special, too out-of-this-world, to wish upon someone else!"

One by one, the girls nodded.

"Fuck it!" said Kat. "Let's keep 'em."

Supper was cooked and eaten with lots of chatter, followed by lounging, wine, and reading. The sun had dropped, the sky a dark indigo by the time the cats came home. They scratched at the door. Maddy jumped up.

"How did you get through the front doors?" she asked as they all rushed in.

Tabby's big voice rose above the sound of scampering paws. "I buzzed the concierge."

The girls gave each other incredulous looks and chuckled.

"I'm going to bed," said Bee. "G'night, babes. G'night cats."

The girls echoed her good wishes and the cats meowed theirs. Maddy lingered, mulling over her day. A few cats crawled into her lap and nuzzled against her hand, fishing for petting.

"Aren't you cuddly all of a sudden?" she said, caressing one little white kitten. She brushed back its fur over its little head.

"What's this? You're dirty." She grabbed a napkin from under her wine glass and spat on a corner, then rubbed reddish crust out of the kitten's whiskers and chin. It came off, but left dark, rust-coloured stains on the cat and napkin. She looked at Tabby, who sat on the couch across from her. His face fur was long, resembling a moustache and beard, making him look older than the others. This goatee of his was covered in the same reddish grime. Maddy's eyes swept over the rest of them; they all had dirty faces. Something was off; but then, she thought, none of this could be considered normal.

The kitten rubbed its head under her hovering hand, which still clutched the damp napkin. She petted it softly, tickling its fluffy belly. Before long, she had drifted off to sleep, hedged in with furballs.

From that day on, Maddy and Jack saw each other every day. During Jack's lunch hour, they would eat, talk for a bit, and make out, each day permitting themselves a little more fondling and one or two fewer items of clothing. By the end of the week, they had moved on to more serious levels of eroticism.

"Can't we move to the bedroom and lock them out?" Jack asked, eyeing the cats with a frown. "Why are we always on the couch?"

"Because it feels spontaneous. And the cats watching kind of turns me on."

"That's fucked up."

Maddy shrugged. "Yeah, I guess so."

Jack looked up; he was sure he'd heard a chuckle somewhere in the room.

"I don't know, Maddy."

"Come on Jack." She pulled him closer. "Try to see them as an aphrodisiac. Play along." And so he did, and they finally made love, on the couch, all the cats watching. But the cats did more than that. They climbed around their naked bodies, purring, rubbing their heads on the lovers' arms, their legs, their feet, their heads if they could. They gave them little bites, to which Maddy responded with stifled moans. Jack would just yelp and jerk, bringing an interesting irregularity to the mix. Their climaxes were accompanied by loud meows, the whole pride partaking in the joyful completion.

Afterwards, the cats paced the apartment, restless.

"Can cats sense when there's a storm coming?" asked Jack, watching them, sweaty, suspicious, but satisfied.

"I don't know." Maddy followed the cats with her eyes, lingering on each one, surprised by the affection she felt for them. Finally, Jack put his clothes back on, gave Maddy a long kiss, and stood, promising to come back on Monday. They at least needed to keep their weekends free from each other, Maddy said, or they'd drive each other nuts in no time. Plus, Saturday was always reserved for curing Friday night's hangover.

And Friday night it was. Once all the dinner things were cleared away, Kat announced that, this evening, they would play poker.

Lo perked up. "Strip?"

"You sound way too excited about that," laughed Kat, raising her eyebrows. "I was thinking we could gamble."

"So you want to play for money," said Bee.

"No, not for money. Things we already have, or favours."

"Favours!" said Lo as she clapped her hands and bounced in her seat.

"I'm in," said Bee. "Maddy, what about you? You seem distracted."

Lo grinned and rolled her eyes. "Maddy has a certain boyfriend on her mind!"

"Oh, that's true!" said Bee. They leaned in, clearly expecting some juicy details.

Maddy turned, her face expressionless, and gestured slowly to the couch. "Well. If you'll cast your eyes downwards; we did it on the couch today. This one." She poked the couch on either side of her.

The girls howled.

"And?" Lo leaned in closer.

"It was great. It was … different."

"Oh, nice. What did you do?" Kat was on the edge of her seat.

"The cats. They were very much involved."

Bee snorted.

Kat looked incredulous. "What?! How?"

So Maddy explained, and they all expressed their jealousy at the feline sexual experience.

"Cats are so sweet. They really feel what we're feeling, don't they?" said Lo.

"I don't know about that," said Kat. "But these ones seem to. We have the smartest, most perverted cats in the world."

Drinks were fixed, poured, and distributed; bras unsnapped; and shoes kicked off. The first thing in the pot was a back rub, and Kat upped the ante to a full body rub. She won with two kings, and the lowest hand to not fold got to be the rub-giver, which was Lo. If everyone folded, the winner chose who would give the favour. Kat kept track of the evening's winnings in her notepad.

Various house chores were collected by each of them, meal preparation and grocery shopping included. Bee lost a pearl necklace to Maddy, and Maddy lost her favourite pair of jean shorts to Kat.

"Worst game ever," she said, bringing her third glass of Jack Daniel's to her lips when, all at once, a wave of nausea hit her. "Fuck. I feel sick."

"What's this?"

She swayed, blinking in the suddenly dazzling light. "I think I'm done for the night, girls."

"You're kidding."

Maddy kissed the girls one after the other, grabbed her new pearl necklace, and dragged her feet all the way into her bedroom. The cats, one and all, followed her.

"Whoa, the sex really got to those cats," said Bee. "Look at them following her. They think she's a goddess."

"A pleasure goddess," said Lo, smiling.

"Do we keep playing?" asked Kat.

"Sure," said Bee. And so they did, gaining and losing various forms of their love and dignity throughout the night.

Maddy was the first to wake, this time without the usual headache that had come as loyally as the sunrise each Saturday morning for the past three years. She kicked the tangled blanket away, covering a few stretched-out cats cuddled among her bedsheets. Her feet searched for a feline-free space on the floor before stepping down, and then tip-toed through more furballs up to her door. Those of the little beasts who were awake rose and followed her into the kitchen, rubbing against her legs as she went. When she sat, a steaming cup of coffee in hand, a few climbed up onto her lap, while others hopped onto the table and observed her through the steam, purring.

"You guys have to chill out," she said. "You're going to drive me up the walls."

The purring stopped. Tabby, who was on the floor, paw leaning on a high-heeled boot, meowed, and the cats swarmed to him. In a huddle, they voiced their usual purrs, meows, weird trills, and grunts. There was also a beep.

"Ray," said Tabby, and they padded off to the front door. Maddy got up and opened it for them, allowing them access to the hallway once more and to whatever adventure they had planned. Whatever it was, it didn't seem to involve smothering Maddy, and for that she was grateful.

The cats didn't come back all week. Consequently, Maddy and Jack's couch escapades lacked a certain edge. Instead, they became gentler and more intimate. That was good too, Maddy supposed. Once, she even invited Jack to her bedroom. Jack told her that he loved her. Maddy said she thought so too.

After work late on Friday afternoon, Bee, Lo, and Kat arrived with their arms full of the usual. The cats trailed behind them like a ball gown train.

"Look at what the girls dragged in," said Bee, the furry critters running past them and leaping onto the couch to cuddle up with Maddy.

"Wow, they sure missed you," said Lo.

"Ya, well, I'm not in the mood," said Maddy, pushing them away and getting up. She walked into the kitchen and began unpacking the shopping bags.

"What's going on?" asked Bee, helping her. "Did you break up with Jack?"

"No," answered Maddy, shoving bags of dried pasta onto the shelves. She pulled out the milk and yogurt, throwing open the fridge without looking at Bee. Lo and Kat were now standing in the kitchen's entryway, watching their upset friend slam cans down and shove drawers shut. Maddy stopped and stared back, her hands on her hips. No one spoke until, at last, tears filled Maddy's eyes. Her hands dropped to her sides.

"I'm pregnant," she said, bursting into sobs. The girls rushed to her, whispering *it's okays*, though, at that moment, no one knew if it really was. Soon the cats were circling them, contributing to the consolation. Holding each other tight, the girls walked with small, obstructed steps all the way to the couches, all of them plopping down on the same one.

"I don't even know if I love him," said Maddy. "It's too soon. I should end it."

"The relationship?" asked Lo, though she knew that wasn't what Maddy had meant.

"The pregnancy," said Maddy.

The cats wailed at the words, hissing even, hackles raised.

"What the fuck is up with them?" asked Kat.

"I don't know," said Maddy. "But they're getting annoying as hell."

"Look," said Lo. "You don't have to make a decision right now. You can think about it."

"If I'm going to put an end to it, I don't want to wait."

The cats hissed again, and Maddy scowled at them.

"Well, at least sleep on it," said Bee.

Maddy nodded. Their quiet supper was peppered with sympathetic smiles and tender, loving touches. Maddy retired early, skipping out on the festivities once again. The girls stayed up a short while, but kept the volume and the drinking to a minimum.

"What do you think she'll do?" Lo whispered.

"Who knows," Bee said. "But it's her decision and hers alone." She looked at the others, her face set. "We support her no matter what."

The Feast

"No more partying," said Bee.

"A baby," said Lo. "Can you imagine?"

They each took a drink and imagined.

"I think kids are a lot of work," Kat said carefully.

Bee nodded. "We could help her."

"She could stay here and we could all be aunties." Lo giggled.

"Well, there's Jack to consider," said Kat. "If she keeps the baby, Jack will want to be in the picture, don't you think? She might even move in with him."

"Who knows. Even the most decent of guys can be surprisingly cowardly when it comes to fatherhood," said Bee.

The girls looked at her, wondering if she had lived something like this herself and hadn't told them.

"Two girls from work," she said as if reading their minds. "One was pressured into an abortion and the daddy took off on the other. Left town."

"Well, they're not all like that," said Lo.

"We're still all so young." Kat sighed, shook her head, and drained the last of her wine.

"And?" asked Bee.

"And ..." Kat looked at Bee. The love she felt for her, for Lo, for Maddy—the friendship they all shared—was suddenly threatened. Kat nibbled on her bottom lip, trying to unscramble her thoughts.

"I'm realizing that the many years I thought we had left, years of partying and fun, of just us and our wildness, are something that can easily be taken away. Having children and settling down are great—if those are things you want, I mean. But, if it was me ... well, I'd have to choose it. I would rather die than be forced into a situation I don't want for myself. And I know that, for now, true love for you three and you three alone is all I can muster. The rest is dispensable. I could never have a baby right now."

Bee frowned at her. "Well," she said, acid on her tongue, "good thing you're not the one who's pregnant. Look, we are going to support Maddy whatever she decides to do. So you just keep those thoughts to yourself, Kat. This is not about you."

"But it is though. You girls are all I have. First Maddy goes, then it'll be Lo."

Lo gaped. "Hey!"

"Then you. I'll be alone."

"Shit, Kat. This is life. Life happens," said Bee. "We can't control every minute of it. We have to adapt. Nothing is safe and secure. Anything can happen. We could die in our sleep tonight, and what could we do to stop it? Nothing. Let it go and be happy for Maddy, whatever she chooses. We'll always be friends. It'll be different, that's all. If anyone understands what it's like to fear losing you guys, it's me. But there's a budding human inside Maddy right now. Do you get it? She has to decide whether to let it live or die!"

Kat sighed and stared past Bee, her eyes on the distant sky. "Yeah, you're right. I'm just so scared of losing you guys."

Lo stood up and wrapped her arms around the two others. "I'd never let anything come between us. We're family. Blood sisters, remember?"

That night, the cats stayed in the living room, staring at each other, communicating without sound. Tabby finally nodded, and then they too settled down for a few hours of sleep.

Maddy woke just before dawn, the apartment still shrouded in the veil of the lingering night. She stepped out of bed and walked to her bedroom door, easing it open so as to avoid creaking hinges. She scurried to the bathroom, and was about to head back to bed for another few hours when she caught a glimpse of something moving on Kat's bedroom floor. Shadows were swaying in the dark, and a sound—a soft tearing— echoed through the just-open door. Maddy approached and poked her head through the gap.

Kat was lying on the floor. Maddy quickly stepped in and flicked the light on, thinking something bad had happened to her: perhaps a heart attack or an overdose. But it was way worse than that.

Maddy screamed, grasping for the doorframe as her legs gave way. Kat's eyes, open and empty, were staring at the ceiling. Around her, half a dozen blood-covered cats were chewing at the meat around her exposed ribcage, her abdomen already gaping, red and purple innards hanging past splintered white bone.

The cats didn't even bother looking up, though Maddy's scream was shrill and steady. Finally gasping for air, she fell backwards through the doorway and out of the room. Slamming another door open, she saw Bee on her bed, the same expression on her face, another crowd of cats chewing on her legs and arms, her chest cavity entirely empty. Maddy, unable now even to scream, ran to Lo's room. She too lay expressionless and half consumed.

Barrelling through the apartment, body numb, wails bubbling from her throat in heaves, Maddy ran out the door and into the hallway, side-sliding like a speeding car all the way downstairs and out through the front door. She kept running, barefoot and in her pyjamas, her one objective to create distance between her and the carnage.

The sun was just beginning to curls its fingers over the city.

"A phone. I need a phone," she muttered through her steady tears. There was no one around, the city still only waking, no one she could ask for help.

A car. She jumped in front of it, the driver slamming on the brakes and stopping only inches from her. She flew up to his window and slapped it repeatedly.

"Please, sir, can I use your phone? It's an emergency."

The car began rolling away.

"I need to call the police! I need to call an ambulance!" She ran alongside it until it sped off, spitting exhaust in her face.

With blackened soles, Maddy stumbled onto the cold tiles of a coffee shop, the door opened to her only thanks to her persistent banging on the shop window.

"I've been walking … for half an hour," she gasped. "There was an accident … at my place … I needed to rush out … That's why … the pyjamas …"

The employee just stared.

"Can I please use your phone?"

The girl went behind the counter, pushed the landline over to her, and continued to grind coffee for the onslaught of morning customers she was soon to receive.

Maddy hesitated and, instead of calling the police, she called Jack.

"Hello?" he said in a scraggly morning voice.

She burst into tears, garbled words squeezing between her sobs.

"Whoa, whoa, slow down. I didn't understand anything. What do you mean, the cats ate the girls?"

Maddy took a deep breath, swallowing her tears, and lowered her voice. The employee was staring at her.

"It was so horrible, Jack," she said. "Please come get me."

"Okay, stay put. I'm coming."

Maddy fell back into a chair and waited. The coffee girl side-eyed her the whole time, even while calibrating the espresso machine, pulling the upside-down chairs from the tables, and writing the specials on the blackboard. She wordlessly unlocked the front door just as Jack pulled up, and Maddy, who had been trying in vain to stop her body from shaking, thanked her and left.

"Okay, so, tell me again why we aren't calling the cops?" said Jack when Maddy had thrown herself in beside him.

"Because they're going to think I did it." Maddy clicked her seatbelt on.

"And why would they think that?"

"Because the cats will be long gone by the time they show up. They're too smart to get caught."

Maddy blew her nose into the tissue from the box on the dashboard.

"They got caught by you, though," said Jack.

That was true. Why didn't they mind Maddy knowing they were murderers? And why hadn't they eaten her as well?

"Look, it's been, what, an hour?" Jack looked at his watch.

And then Maddy thought of the millions of movies she had watched and the stories she'd read where she'd sworn at the protagonist for not doing the logical thing, the right thing; for getting themselves into more trouble. She didn't want to be that idiot.

"Fine," she said, sniffling. "Let's call the cops."

After crying over the phone as she retold the story at least three times, she was instructed to meet the police in front of the building. Do not go up, they said. Well, she had no intention of going back up—not ever.

Her apartment was only a five-minute drive away, but the police were already there when they rolled up. Two ambulances idled beside them, the sight sending

Maddy's heart into gallops. Her eyes locked onto the building's front door as they waited.

Soon, three stretchers were rolled out, a pair of paramedics to each, a white sheet pulled over the laid-out bodies. Maddy burst into uncontrollable hysterics. Jack tried to hold her, but she cried harder and pushed him away, gasping for air, flailing, drowning.

"Wait here," he said, though he was sure she didn't hear anything. A few minutes later, he came back with a bottle of water and a few pills. "Here, the paramedics said this would calm you down."

Maddy stopped crying and stared at his open hand, then looked up at him.

"I can't take that," she said.

"Why not? It's relax … a … prol, or something. You're over the top. This will take the edge off."

"I'm fine now. See?" She took big, jagged breaths, clutching the sides of her seat.

"Okay, well, I'll put them here if you want them. There's no shame in it, Maddy." Jack dropped the little pills in the built-in change holder on the dashboard.

Maddy was relieved he hadn't pushed the pills on her. She hadn't made a decision about the baby yet, and didn't want to have to tell him now—not like this.

An officer knocked on Jack's window. He rolled it down.

"We need Miss Stacks to identify the bodies," he said to Jack.

"Why didn't he just ask me?" said Maddy. "Does he think you're the boss of me or something?" She stepped out of the car, feeling like a flustered child, and joined the officer at the ambulance.

"I hope you're not squeamish," he said to her. He then nodded to the paramedic, who pulled down the sheet from the first body, exposing the face. The cheeks had been gnawed at, but it was clearly the beautiful Kat. Maddy stifled a sob behind her hand, intent on keeping her shit together. The sheet was pulled back up and they began pushing the body into the ambulance.

"Wait!" yelled Maddy. She leaned over and hugged Kat over the white sheet. "I love you," she whispered through the fabric by her friend's ear. She did the same with Lo, sweet and caring Lo, who was missing part of her nose. And Bee, her face untouched, angelic. She watched them disappear into the faceless vehicles, the stretcher legs folding up behind them, gone forever.

"We need to have a word with you now, Miss Stacks," said the policeman.

Maddy nodded.

She told the story from the beginning, omitting the spacecraft crashing onto the roof. She didn't know why. Probably another protagonist's illogical and idiotic decision, because she had no reason to protect the cats' identities. She told the officer that she and her roommates had come across the cats on their way home one day, that they'd followed them to the door of the building. They'd looked so decrepit and hungry, she said, so they took them in.

It was more believable this way. Besides, if for some reason the craft happened to no longer be on the roof, Maddy could have been joining Jake at the institute. Maybe they'd have even forced her to end her pregnancy. The sudden thought made her defensive, waking a natural urge to protect the baby. It was hers and no one else's. It was all she had left.

She placed her hand on her womb. The flashing lights faded into the periphery, the sound of the officer scribbling on his clipboard pushed into the background. Maddy felt herself compress—into her heart, into a new love she felt there, small, tight, and powerful like an atom she didn't dare split open. She knew then that lying was the right thing for this protagonist to do.

He mentioned the kitty litter being empty and the food bowls full. Maddy didn't comment.

"Well, there's cat hair everywhere in there. And the wounds were unmistakably made by animal claws and teeth. Even so, we'll be running some tests." He flipped down the cover to his clipboard and looked at Maddy, who had her hand in front of her mouth again, shoulders jerking with each strangled sob. "Stay in town, Miss Stacks. We'll be getting in touch soon to let you know when you can go back to your apartment."

Apparently, there'd been no sign of the cats when the cops showed up. A team was promptly sent to search the nearby parks, and another the neighbours' yards and porches. All the tenants in the building had been questioned, but no one had seen the killers, neither before or after the incident.

Over the coming weeks, it blew over as a freak attack. People were warned to monitor their domesticated pets for any abnormal behaviour. Even dogs were placed under scrutiny. But nothing out of the ordinary happened anywhere else. And, since no one wanted to suspect their fur babies, pet owners and others alike quickly moved on and forgot about the vicious triple murder. Everyone but Maddy.

Jack was her rock over the following months, and proved himself to be top-notch boyfriend material. So, when Maddy finally started showing, she told him.

"Why did you wait so long to tell me?" he asked gently.

"I needed to be sure you'd stick around."

She looked down into her mint tea, her eyes reflected perfectly in its dark green surface. They fell into a fragile silence, one that told her she'd been wrong about him. Jack didn't want this child. When she placed her elbow onto the table and her hand over her eyes, he rushed to her side.

"Hey," he said. "I'm not going anywhere."

Heart, Not Blood

Six months into the pregnancy, Maddy moved in with Jack, retrieving only her clothes and a few souvenirs from the apartment she had shared with the girls for the last three years. The rest had been painfully boxed up for the Salvation Army.

They were expecting a girl, as of yet nameless. Maddy continued working from home, though it was very different with no cats to babysit. They had not shown the tips of their noses since that horrible morning, and Maddy had promised that she'd turn them all into ground meat if she ever saw them again. In fact, these days she couldn't stand the sight of any cat whatsoever, and would scream with rage at any stray that happened to cross her path.

As the months passed, Maddy became more and more reclusive. She'd barely left the house in weeks, preferring to stay somewhere she could safely fall apart. Wastebaskets of tissue paper filled and overflowed like fluffy white volcanoes, erupting many times a day, the refuse collected at regular intervals and consigned to a bigger container. Her face was a waterlogged skin-pillow, swollen and threatening to burst at the slightest poke.

She wouldn't see anyone, so Jack had to become everyone—shrink, confidant, comforter, lover, friend, maid, cook, chauffeur, masseuse, hairdresser. He couldn't keep up. Drained of his energy, his skin shrivelled like a prune and his eyes sunk into his head like a hazelnut on a collapsed tart. Their faces were complete opposites, as were becoming their hearts.

Seven months into Maddy's pregnancy, Jack was hit by a truck while riding his bicycle to work. It wasn't a mango truck but, oddly, it *was* a fruit truck. He died from his wounds that night, and Maddy vowed to never eat fruit again. Her last childbearing weeks were spent in the poorest of health, and the baby came early, keen to take her ticket out of the depressed, filthy, and strictly chocolate-fed mother.

The small body was out in three pushes, Maddy finding strength in anger. Once the head and shoulders were through, the creature slipped out the rest of the way. The tiny mewling thing was handed to the mother.

But Maddy turned her head away.

"Miss Stacks, your baby," said the nurse, a chime of joy in her voice, thinking Maddy zoned out from fatigue.

Maddy forced her head to turn in the direction of the nurse, who was already placing the goopy baby on her bare chest. She swallowed down hard and looked at the lump of damp flesh. It felt separate from her, a thing that her body had made during the worst months of her life. Reluctantly, Maddy gave the child her breast, feeling a tinge of revulsion at the neediness it already expressed just by existing.

"Have you a name for the child, Miss Stacks?" asked the nurse.

"Edie," said Maddy, the name bitter in her mouth. "Her father liked that name best."

After a few days of unenthusiastic childcare and fragmented sleep, mother and child were sent home.

Baby car seat dangling from her bony grip, Maddy stood in the doorway for several minutes, staring at the ruined mess of her home with deep apathy. The car seat placed on the kitchen floor, she let her torpor pull her to the couch, where she sat down, lay her head back, and stared at the ceiling. Hours passed. When she finally rose, she tidied the trash, and then hoisted the baby.

Looking into the big blue eyes that gazed up at her lovingly, Maddy felt nothing. She was paper-thin; without substance. She could hardly stand her own weak pulse, let alone someone else's. She wanted to burn everything down.

But she didn't. Instead, she got used to picking up her mountains of snotty, tear-soaked tissues, feeding herself, and feeding Edie. She never looked at her for too long. Glances, just to make sure everything was in its right place, especially while nursing. God forbid she'd come to love this creature. It would most certainly be ripped away from her, like everything else she'd loved before. No, she took care of Edie because she had to, out of moral obligation, and without feeling. She kept them both safe that way. Safe from the sadness of living, and safe from death.

From the shabby couch, Maddy stared at the fingerprint-ridden glass-top coffee table while baby Edie cried from her crib in the kitchen. She'd gotten good at ignoring the little wails, which often died out in hitched breaths if she waited long enough. This time, though, Edie wasn't calming down. With a heavy sigh, Maddy pushed herself up and dragged her feet across the cold floor of the coldest room in the house.

Lifting the child out by the armpits, she laid it on the cold kitchen table. Its clothes were unbuttoned, its diaper removed, its butt wiped with a cold wet cloth, and, re-wrapped in its layers—mechanically, emotionlessly—the baby was placed back down in the crib. There, it cried.

For years, Maddy mothered with the same coldness as a cuckoo bird. She could easily have dropped Edie off to be cared for by someone who could do it better, but something held her back. Instead, she opted to cover only the basics of survival, while, more often than not, the child's cries for comfort and human warmth went ignored.

That was, until Edie came home from kindergarten one afternoon with her face bloody and dirty, holding a note from the teacher.

"You fell?" Maddy asked Edie.

"Yes, Mother," said Edie, eyes to the floor, hands clasped behind her back.

"*Apply vitamin E ointment. The child doesn't pay attention. Needs to watch where she's going,*" she read. "What? Why didn't she clean you up?"

Edie didn't look up. "I don't know. It's okay, I'm okay."

"It most certainly isn't okay!"

Bypassing all the settings, rust and calcification cracking and crumbling, the switch flicked. Maddy turned ferocious, a deep protective instinct bubbling wildly to the surface. The next day, when she stormed into that little brick piece of shit they called a school, broken child in tow, they told her to calm down. To that, she told them to fuck off and left, still holding the little wrist tight in her grip.

She took Edie home. That day, Maddy dared to feel something other than a lifeless sense of duty. A flicker of warmth came to life, an ember just strong enough to spark a small flame of remorse. This was not a new feeling for her; she'd felt tsunamis of it since the passing of everyone she loved. Remorse for not having been kinder to her parents while they'd still been alive; remorse for having sucked the life out of Jack (the fruit truck, she knew, had just finished him off); remorse for not having been eaten by the cats along with her friends.

But now, for the first time, she felt like she could do something about this remorse. Edie was still young, and the damage could be remedied. At least, she hoped it could.

The decision was to be more significant for Maddy than for Edie—at first, anyway. She planned to adopt another child so that Edie would have someone, a sibling, to love her. Because, no matter the flicker of warmth or the depth of her remorse, Maddy could not conjure and nor would she permit herself to feel that sentiment ever again.

An older girl whose parents had died in a car crash had been waiting for many months to be taken into a proper home. Maddy knew this child was to be pitied, just like her own, and figured they'd be a good match for each other. Her name was Emily. And, very unexpectedly, Maddy grew to love her.

Thinking it was her only chance to win back her humanity, Maddy indulged in her revived emotions, showering this new child with gifts and a growing amount of awkward affection. Emily was kind and patient, the suffering brought by the loss of her parents blessing her with gentleness and humility. Although Emily would often shoot sidelong glances in Edie's direction when her adoptive mother squeezed her, knowing full well that Edie was never so lucky, no rivalry came of it. The look was one of pity. Young Emily often attempted to hug her little sister, the desire to do so arising naturally, but she was always pushed away by a child increasingly indifferent to the whole idea of closeness.

A creative urge as surprising as love itself arose next in Maddy's heart, one so strong that she was compelled to finish the story she had started the night of Jake's abduction. She returned to the beginning, starting with the blood oath. It would serve, she thought, as a warning for her children. But she kept writing, way past the adoption of Emily, and doing so scared her, for she didn't approve of what she was writing. It became wilder as it went, full of suffering, substance abuse, and debauchery. All the evil she wanted to save her children from flowed onto the page and, afraid she'd bring these events into the real world, just as she had once upon a time, she burned the pages one by one. There would be no allegory.

Maddy raised her children carefully, sharing her wisdom and opinions liberally, especially regarding one subject: Sex. Fornication. Lovemaking. Every form at any time. It was all bad, she told them, "and leads only to trouble." Heartbreak or pregnancy; neither was desirable. Chastity alone would secure her children's wellbeing and happiness.

Her admonitions were heard but not heeded.

Emily married young, pure and sinless, her romantic dreams unsullied by her mother's pessimism, and Edie, an uncontrollable teenager, full of fire and seeking to fill the holes in her forsaken heart, slipped and slid off the straight and narrow that had been paved for her. She would spend the rest of her life bouncing between the cruellest and most jealous partners the world had to offer.

With Emily gone, home became a claustrophobia-inducing box of yelling, door slamming, and interminable silent treatments. The glitter from her graduation ceremony and subsequent ball still clinging to her skin, Edie took off with nothing but a backpack and a hardened, flaking pride.

With no anchor to keep it steady, Maddy's heart caught the wind and was launched out into the open sea. The protective walls it had built around itself crashed down upon themselves, and destructive, unbridled emotion came flooding in, drowning everything in saltwater. And so it was that, a week after Edie jumped ship, Maddy left the world.

Her duty as a mother, however badly done, was complete. She joined Lorraine, Beatrice, and Katherine. She was greeted by Jack, the loyal and radiant angel full of understanding. And her parents, they were there as well, waiting to greet her as loving pencils of light. And the physical world seemed then insignificant—wholly, if not for its true substance: the souls that inhabited it. The souls that struggled through the grime and grit of life, that rejoiced and exulted in its many gifts. She could see Edie, if she wanted to.

"Don't you dare," Darrell said, staring her down, finger pointing and stale beer on his breath. "Don't you dare step out that door!"

Her backpack flung over her shoulder, Edie pushed the screen door open. Before her foot hit the porch, she was yanked backwards, the man with the finger and the breath dragging her down the hallway, the backpack straps burning her underarms as she clawed at the walls and floor. He threw her into the bedroom.

"Look, Edie," he said, catching his breath, "I only hurt you because I love you. You're the person I'm the closest to in this world. Don't you understand? I'm sorry it's come to this."

Edie picked herself up and poised herself to run, her eyes on the doorway, ignoring the same speech she'd heard a hundred times before. Darrell blocked her path, anticipating her next move. She lunged anyway. The blow that slammed into her cheek was expected, just as every other she'd received from him had been. She crumbled to the floor. Darrell, at this point, would usually crumble down beside her and cradle her in his arms, begging for forgiveness. Instead, he kicked her in the stomach.

"You know what?" he said, standing over her as she gasped for breath. "Fucking leave. *Now!*"

Edie struggled to her feet, grabbed her bag, and ran.

And ran.

And ran.

Edie didn't cry. Bitterness and distrust were the only fruit she'd ever known; the harvest she deserved, apparently, for the life she was leading. Why was she here, on this earth? She often asked herself that question. But not once had she thought of leaving the depressing and filthy body of the world. Because, somehow, she was still whole. Against the odds. And, despite everything, she counted herself lucky. Having grown strangely resilient, she harboured the hope that eventual happiness could one day be hers, so long as she kept to herself.

And so, from that day on, Edie cut herself off. It wasn't so different—she'd always been alone, after all, on the inside.

At the funeral, Edie gave a flat smile as Emily approached with open arms. Though she let her adopted sister hug her, she didn't reciprocate the affection. In fact, it had taken years of concerted effort on Emily's part for them to share anything that could faintly qualify as a relationship. It was small, but it was enough to satisfy Emily and just enough for Edie to feel like she had some kind of family. In the end, Edie knew, family didn't fall to blood, but to heart.

The two dozen cats stayed in town, working with Ray, the dry-cleaning clerk, trying to get something from him that he just didn't have. But they didn't give up. They had time. They ate when they had to and, having learned their lesson, did so conspicuously. It was easy enough to consume a whole body, bones included.

Still, they had left quite the mess that day at the Dugger's Mental Health Institute. Poor Jake had just gotten settled into a room with its own bathroom and cable television. His first meal had been left untouched in its plastic tray—perched on the table across from Cliff Clavin and Woody Boyd, who sipped vacantly on pints—so quick were the cats to get to him. The incident hadn't even been mentioned in the news. People there came and went, sometimes a little more violently than others. He'd been claimed by his family, though, who were left with a whole litany of unanswered questions. Poor Jake had walked right into Maddy's plot and had ended up as kitty fodder, slowly paving the way for the coming of Edie.

Edie, made special from voyeurism and kitten bites.

Edie, who'd have a long road ahead before she meandered into the happiness she had imagined only in her dreams.

Edie, who had no idea that her dreadful beginnings would guide her safely through the chaos that awaited her.

Maddy, from behind the veil, finally learned to love her daughter. She kept her eyes on her.

And so did the cats.

ACKNOWLEDGEMENTS

I'd like to thank coffee, snacks, and my husband's fear of cats for propelling me along on this little feline adventure. Also big-as-the-sky thanks those who've read Crash Kitty and/or Off my Feet in their early stages—Johnna, Geneviève, Steffi, Lien, Pierre, Verna, Mitch, Tuesday Rain—and have helped me have the confidence to just be myself, and write like myself, even if it rocks the boat. Or, especially if it rocks the boat. I thank the tough love of editors, as much as it can be hard, I grow each time. A heartfelt thanks to those who buy books written by indie authors like myself. It's a tricky path for us, one that requires courage and self-confidence, know-how and resourcefulness, and a lot of help from friends. And still we shake in our boots, even though DIY is punk to the core. Because we bypassed the gatekeeper. We forged our own way. Crossing our fingers and squeezing our eyes shut, we wait to see if the world will be the same when we open them. Personally, I sure hope not.

ABOUT THE AUTHOR

My name is Rachel(le) Tremblay and I'm a writer, painter, and musician from Montreal, Canada. I'm the result of a spiritual upbringing by rock n' rollers, a childhood of hair metal, Seattle grunge, California punk rock, east coast hip hop, horror movies, guitar shredding, skateboarding and poetry. I married young and I homeschool(ed) my kids. They're my favourite people. I love sneakers, comfy jeans, tattoos, and low-maintenance braids. Cinnamon gum. Authenticity. Kindness. That sort of thing. Kindness never gets old.

Other Books by Rachel Tremblay

Off My Feet (adult)
The Nirvana Threads (NA / adult)
Topaz: The Truth Portal & The Color Mayhem (all ages)

www.rachel-tremblay.com